The Flying Ferry Boat

An Amazing

San Francisco Adventure

By Judy Reynolds Dumm

Judy Reynolds Dumm

Edited by Cathy Vertuca

Illustrated by Timothy Allen Estrada

Library of Congress Catalog Card Number: 97-09153
ISBN: 0-9637217-0-4

Additional copies of this book may be ordered from:
Peak Experience Arts & Publishing
P.O. Box 2116
Santa Rosa, CA 95405-0116

Printed by Barlow Printing
Cotati, California

First Printing July, 1997

This book is dedicated to my grandparents
Donald S. and M. Juanita Jordan

and written for my granddaughters
Ariel and Alyssa Kent

"Daddy, who pulls the plug to clean San Francisco Bay?"

When my mother's family moved to the Bay Area in the 1920s, there were no bridges across San Francisco Bay. A favorite family activity was to ride the big white ferryboat from Oakland to San Francisco. The highlights of the trip for the four children were to feed bread to the seagulls and to jump around shrieking when the ferryboat's horn blew its deep blast. On one of these rides my Uncle Don, the youngest child, noticed some green scum coating the edge of the Bay and asked, "Daddy, who pulls the plug to clean San Francisco Bay?" After all, his mother pulled the plug in their tub at home and scrubbed it clean after his bath. My grandfather didn't answer the question that day, but soon began weaving a series of tall tales that included the story of the Flying Ferry Boat.

A fond memory of mine is sitting on my grandfather's knee listening to him create a new adventure with his own spectacular sound effects. I wanted to preserve these stories for our family. When I started collecting them, I found that each generation and each family remembered tales that no one else had heard. I have intertwined many of the stories to make one continuous adventure, updating them with some additions of my own. After I shared my completed manuscript with some friends, I realized that children who visit or live near San Francisco might also enjoy knowing about the Flying Ferry Boat.

If you are reading this story aloud, I encourage you to add sound effects to help return this tale to the tradition of oral story-telling, experiencing it as I once did. Now, climb on board the Flying Ferry Boat for an amazing San Francisco adventure.

TABLE OF CONTENTS

1   Wishing for a Friend 1

2   Ready for Lift-Off 13

3   Into the Depths of the Bay 29

4   Collision Course 51

5   His Majesty, King Crab 61

6   King Crab's Royal Palace............. 75

7   Fisherman's Wharf and
      Ghirardelli Square 93

8   Pulling the Plug 107

9   A Dangerous Rescue 123

10 Flying to the North Pole 133

11 Hey, We Cleaned Up the Bay!.... 153

12 Farewell to Joe 'Dobe 169

      Complete Activities List............. 182

San Francisco Bay Area and Beyond

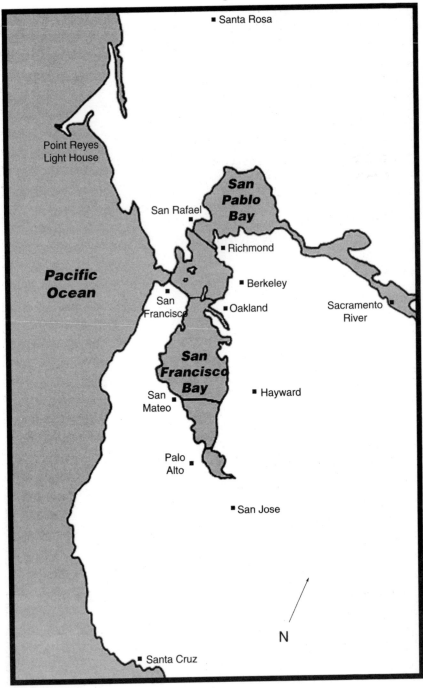

Santa Rosa

Point Reyes
Light House

San Pablo Bay

San Rafael

Richmond

Pacific Ocean

Berkeley

San Francisco

Oakland

Sacramento River

San Francisco Bay

Hayward

San Mateo

Palo Alto

San Jose

N

Santa Cruz

Close-up View of the San Francisco Bay Area

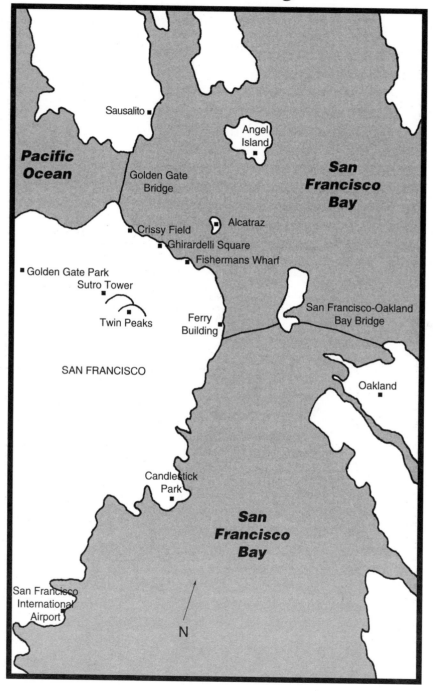

Chapter 1

Wishing for a Friend

The seventeenth of October was an Indian summer day in the Santa Cruz Mountains. It was hot and very still. "Perfect earthquake weather," the old-timers would say.

The clock over the fireplace at the Jordan's new home chimed 5:00 PM. It was time for the World Series to start and Donald was really looking forward to the game. He had been wearing his new Giants baseball cap and tee-shirt all day. He and his dad were comfortably seated on the couch in front of the television. They nibbled buttery popcorn from a big bowl and waited for the pregame show to be over.

Suddenly the earth began to shake. The ground moved gently at first, then rolled up and down. The windows of the house rattled, the living room couch joggled back and forth, and the light fixture over the dining room table swung from side to side. Donald's mother frantically yelled from the kitchen, "This must be an earthquake. Hurry, get outside!"

Donald grabbed the bowl of popcorn and raced out the front door. He could barely stay on his feet because the ground under him moved like a rocking boat. His stomach flip-flopped and he felt seasick. The young boy's body trembled with fear and his legs seemed as if they had turned to jelly. Donald was almost ten years old and had never been so frightened in his life. Now he was too scared to do anything, so he just sat down. He wished he was younger because then he wouldn't feel embarrassed if he held someone's hand.

In the next few seconds he watched as the asphalt driveway *craaaacked.* The whole house shifted and the roof *craaaashed* into the rooms below. At the same moment, the tall Redwood trees leaned as the force of the quake moved their roots. One tree *smaaaashed* onto the garage.

The violent shaking seemed to go on forever, but it really only lasted thirty seconds. Coming slowly to his feet, Donald took a wide-eyed look at the damage. His parents were as dazed as he was, saying little as they wandered around the wreckage.

The house had moved off its foundation, sliding to the south. Pieces of the roof poked through the broken windows and the house kept making strange *creeeeaking* noises as things settled inside. The trunk of an enormous Redwood tree lay on their cars, completely crushing them. A narrow crack ran across their driveway and the ground on either side had split open as well. Sirens sounded in the distance.

Everything was ruined. There was no electricity or telephone. Donald's video games, his computer and his Legos were buried under the caved-in roof. The boy felt devastated.

It wasn't that long ago that Donald and his family had moved to this new home in the middle of twenty acres. He had heard about the earthquakes in California, but nothing prepared him for this. Right now he wanted to be back in his old neighborhood in Kansas with friendly neighbors close by and ground that never moved.

The sun dropped lower and lower in the sky. It was dinner time, but the only food they had was the bowl of cold popcorn. They shared it in silence, barely tasting the salty kernels. As it got darker the family swung into action and got their camping gear out of the tool shed. They pitched a tent, blew up their air mattresses and unrolled the sleeping bags. Soon they had a sparse camp set up in their front yard.

Donald was cold and tired. He wished he could sleep in his own bed under his cozy quilt. Instead, he crawled into the tent with his parents and zipped up his sleeping bag. He tried to sleep, but was frequently shaken awake by the aftershocks. These mini-earthquakes caused him to shiver with fear, and in the eerie silence of night, the boy had nightmares.

When they awoke the next morning, a cold, drizzling rain was falling. Everything was soaking wet and the soil in their yard had turned into mud—a heavy, reddish-brown mud called adobe. (Pronounced *a-doe'-bee*.) Whenever Donald entered the tent, gobs of sticky adobe came with him.

"Wipe your shoes before you come in here!" his mom shouted.

"Don't sit on your sleeping bag in those muddy jeans," his dad hollered.

"Keep out of that mud! Can't you do anything right, Donald?" His parents were very cranky and complained more than usual. They grouched at their son because no one else was around.

Donald was unhappy and very lonely. He had been sad when he left his good friends in the Midwest and he was just beginning to make new friends in Santa Cruz. Now his school was closed because of the earthquake damage.

At first he worked with his parents removing some of their belongings from the house and clearing away as much debris as they could. After a few days Donald decided it was best to stay out of their way, so he looked for something else to do. Eventually the mud became his entertainment. He ran and slid in it, squishing it under his boots. He built tiny villages with mud mountains, dirt roads, lakes full of water and mud buildings. He made adobe mud balls and threw them at a target. Fortunately his parents had stopped bugging him about getting muddy, since there was mud covering every inch of their yard

Lying on his sleeping bag one night, Donald said out loud, "I need a friend." His imagination began to wander. After some time an idea came to him. "I know, I'll make a friend out of mud. In Kansas I made a snowman, so why don't I make a California mudman?"

He tried to talk to his parents about his idea. "I want to build a mudman. How big do you think I could make him? Where should I build him? Would mud really work like snow? What do you think? . . . Dad? . . . Mom?" There was no answer. His parents were so tired, they had already fallen asleep.

The next day Donald was again eager to talk about his plans. "Dad, I have a great idea."

In a hurry to get something else done, his dad replied, "Do whatever you want, son. You're on your own until the house is repaired."

Determined to really build a man, Donald experimented with the clay-like soil. He pulled a water hose to a level place far away from the house and dampened the ground, then began patting large mudballs into shape. He soon discovered that the adobe needed to have exactly the right amount of water to stay firm. He also found that when the mudball dried too much, he had to sprinkle it with water so new layers of adobe could be added. Donald made several big reddish-brown mudballs and left them to harden in the sun while he drew an outline of a gigantic man in the soft dirt. By dinner time, he was certain that his plan would work.

The next morning Donald enthusiastically began his project, talking as he worked. "I want you to be the biggest and best friend possible. I want you to be strong. I want you to have big arms to hug me and soft hands to hold when I'm afraid. I'll give you a friendly face so you can smile at me and big ears so you can listen to me."

He got busy and formed two enormous feet, as big as king-sized pillows. He carefully sculpted extra-large toes that looked something like his small ones. By the end of the day, the boy's hands were raw from scraping mud off the ground. He knew he needed some tools and a better way to get a large amount of adobe.

The following morning Donald awoke and ate a quick breakfast. In the tool shed, he found a pair of work gloves that almost fit him. He also pulled out a shovel, buckets and a tall ladder and hauled everything to his work site. Then he dug a pit and filled it with water. He added adobe soil a shovelful at a time, mixing it until it thickened. Soon he had an ample supply of mud that was just right.

The energetic boy began mounding buckets of soft mud on the fat feet. *Goooosh. Goooosh. Goooosh.* It took two days of hard work to construct the solid set of legs he figured his friend would need. After the warm sunshine hardened them, he smiled and commented, "Now you have two extra-large, extra-fat, trash barrel-sized legs."

Next, Donald needed to build the body. He set the ladder beside the two plump legs. Filling a small bucket with adobe mud, he climbed up and dumped all the gooey mixture on top of the legs. *Goooosh.* He went up the ladder again and again, layering bucketfuls of soft adobe on the growing body. *Goooosh. Goooosh.* When the inside layers got hard, he began gently shaping the outer layers of mud into a fat bottom, round stomach, big back, broad chest and sloping shoulders.

As the body grew, Donald patted small handfuls of mud here and there to make his man look strong and muscular. Instead, the muddy sculpture appeared to have dimples and bumps everywhere, but the boy liked his creation because it was different from any he had ever seen. He laughed and said, "Man, you're so lumpy. You're beginning to look like you're stuffed full of potatoes."

The arms were next. To give them strength, Donald stuck two tree branches deep into each side of the body and positioned them so the man would have his hands on his hips. He applied layer after layer of mud around the branches until the arms were strong and solid. Donald was pleased that his idea worked so well and was certain that a bear hug from those big arms would feel great.

Lying in his sleeping bag that night, he thought about making two wonderful hands with fat fingers. This time he decided to use a framework of forked twigs so the mud would again have something to mold around. Satisfied with this idea, he drifted to sleep.

Before starting to work the next morning, Donald spoke to his silent mudman. "I had a crazy dream last night. You came to life and took me someplace far away. I held your hand and I felt safe. Today I'm going to make you some great hands, the kind I want to hold when I'm scared."

After gathering his sticks, adding water to the pit and stirring the adobe, he set to work molding one finger at a time. It wasn't as easy as he thought it would be, but Donald worked hours and hours until he had made two amazingly lifelike hands resting on the figure's wide hips.

On his next workday, Donald climbed all the way up his ladder. Leaning on the solid mud body for support, he asked his sculpture, "How large should your head be?" In a minute he answered himself. "The size of my Halloween pumpkin should be about right." He moistened the top of the torso and built a thick neck. Then he hauled up several big buckets of mud and slowly shaped a large, bald head.

"Now, how about your face?" he questioned out loud. "Do you want a big nose or a little one like mine? Should your eyes be close together or far apart? What kind of a smile do you want? How big should your ears be?" Using his pocketknife, the boy began carving. He sculpted a sharp nose, tiny eyes, a slight smile and small, rounded ears.

Donald went down the ladder and stepped back to look at his creation. He was very disappointed. "Oh, no! Your face doesn't look like the mudman in my dream at all." He hauled up another bucketful of mud and carefully covered the first face. "I'm going to start all over," he told his man.

He tried to picture the grinning giant in his mind and thoughtfully remade the face. This time he formed a broad smile, widely spaced eyes and a fat, pudgy nose. He gave him big ears that stuck out from the sides of his head. To complete his mudman's appearance, the boy added a double chin and put a twist of grassy hair on the top of the bald head.

Jumping back to the ground, Donald announced, "That's it! That's exactly the face I remember. Now you look like the man I saw in my dream!" Proud of himself, he rushed to find his parents. "Hey, Mom! Hey, Dad! I finished him. Come and see my mud friend."

By now the adobe man stood as high as the eves on the house and looked quite lifelike. Donald's parents were amazed at the mud sculpture. His mom stared up at the enormous smiling figure and complimented her son. "We didn't know you were such a creative boy. Your man looks so real."

"Now he needs a name. Any ideas, Mom?" Donald asked.

"Well, if you had made a mudwoman," his mom declared, "you could have named her Muddy Maude."

"But he's a man, so what do you think about calling him Adobe Man?" Donald asked.

"Good idea," his mom remarked.

"Adobe Joe sounds good to me," his dad

chimed in.

Donald thought about it carefully. "Hmm, Joe Adobe..." Suddenly a similar name popped into his head and he made the decision easily. "I dreamed about him last week and now I remember—his name is Joe 'Dobe."

"Not a bad name for a hunk of adobe mud," his dad agreed.

After his parents returned to their chores, Donald spoke to the jumbo mudman who was lifeless in the early evening light. "Hello, up there. I'm Donald, you know, and you're Joe 'Dobe, right? Isn't that what you told me in my dream?" The mudman winked at him. Or at least Donald thought he winked. Squinting, Donald asked, "Joe 'Dobe, did you wink at me? Are you alive? Could you talk to me?"

He reached up and put his small hand in the large mud hand. It was cold and hard. Donald closed his eyes and wished his friend was alive. He felt safe and happy next to his giant man. "Good night, Joe 'Dobe," he said gently. "See you in the morning."

Suggested Activity: *Get some clay and sculpt a mud person you would like for a friend. Or just try making a great hand to hold. If you are in certain areas of the Santa Cruz Mountains, you will find adobe clay in the ground.*

11

Chapter 2

Ready for Lift-Off

Donald had trouble going to sleep that dark Halloween Eve. He was excited about finishing his mudman, but something else was keeping him awake. Strange thoughts that Joe 'Dobe had really winked at him continued to float through his mind.

He was sound asleep when he felt a weak tug on the foot of his sleeping bag. The pull was so gentle that it awakened only him. Peering into the darkness he saw a slight movement. With his heart pounding, he slipped on his jeans and tennis shoes. He grabbed his sweat shirt and baseball cap and quickly stepped outside.

"Who is it?" he whispered.

"Shhhhh. Don't . . . uh, be afraid," a low, rumbling voice slowly said. "It's me, Joe 'Dobe. Come on!"

Joe extended a warm, soft hand and gently led Donald away from the tent. Puzzled, the boy whispered, "Joe 'Dobe? Really? You're alive? Wow! Hey, did you wink at me last night?"

"Uh, . . . yup," was the hushed answer.

They went quietly down the long driveway

and turned on to a trail. As they started through the woods, Donald asked, "Where are we going?"

Joe 'Dobe answered slowly, "I . . . uh, wanted you to meet . . . uh, Captain Nimbo." Still holding Donald's hand, he guided him through the early morning darkness, stumbling down the long narrow path.

"Who's Captain Nimbo?"

"My . . . uh, sea captain friend," Joe stuttered.

"What? How could that be? I just built you."

"You'll see," the mudman said, not being able to think very fast. Suddenly Joe 'Dobe tripped. "Oops."

"Be careful," Donald cautioned.

"I'm . . . a clumsy guy. Yup, I am," Joe remarked with a deep chuckle. "Donald, I . . . uh, want to thank you for bringing me back to life. I . . . thought the best way to do that might be . . . uh, to take you on a short trip . . . and let you see some of the rest of the world."

Not quite understanding what Joe meant, Donald held on to the mudman's soft hand as they walked across a meadow. Then, unexpectedly, the boy saw something in front of them. It seemed to be an enormous two-storied white house suspended over the grass. Donald's grip on Joe 'Dobe's hand tightened. "What's that?" he asked.

Before Joe 'Dobe could answer, an extremely tall, thin man carrying a kerosene lantern appeared in front of them. He wore old-fashioned wool sailor pants that were too short and a shabby pullover sweater. In the lantern light Donald could see his bent wire-framed glasses, a gold earring glimmering from his left ear and a wooden pipe clenched between his teeth. When he saw them he hollered, "Ahoy there, Joe 'Dobe!"

Unsure of the whole situation, Donald hid behind the mudman. He peeked around the big legs to check out the stranger and the mysterious white *whatever it was*.

Joe's voice boomed, "Captain Nimbo, it's good to see you again!" He stumbled forward and gave his old friend a big bear hug.

The captain complained, "Watch it there, you clumsy clod of mud. You're squeezing the breath out of me!"

" Sorry, . . . I forget how strong I am . . . and you know I fall over my big feet." Joe's conversation continued to be slow and awkward. "Thanks . . . for coming to meet us. Is . . . uh, the ferryboat ready?"

Pointing his pipe at the white structure, the captain answered, "This old bag of timbers? Sure, she's always ready to shove off. I was just waiting for you."

"Well, I'm here and so is the . . . uh, kid who rebuilt me," Joe 'Dobe said, searching his brain for the words he needed.

"Kid? What kid?" the captain questioned, squinting into the darkness.

"Donald, why are you hiding? Come, meet the captain." Joe 'Dobe reached behind him

and easily scooped up the young boy. He slowly introduced them. "Captain Nimbo, . . . meet Donald Jordan. And Donald, this is . . . the captain of the one and only Flying Ferry Boat."

Dangling from Joe's strong arms, Donald managed to say hello. He noticed that the captain was skinny as a flagpole, with curly hair bushing out from beneath his old white hat. On his weather-beaten face he had a wiry beard, with patches of gray around his chin. But what really captured Donald's attention was the huge boat looming in front of them. Amazed, he asked, "Wow, is this really a ferryboat?"

Captain Nimbo answered, "Aye, aye. It's the ferryboat that used to carry cars and trucks across the Bay during the 1920s. We ran every hour from Oakland to San Francisco before the bridges were built. She's my home. Joe used to live on her too, before he tripped one too many times and fell overboard." The captain chomped impatiently on his pipe stem. "Well, come on, Joe. Let's get going. Shove off, kid."

Joe scratched his head, thinking hard. "Captain, . . . Donald is . . . uh, coming with us," he stated.

"Just a minute, Joe. No young, inexperienced, know-nothing, *landlubber* is setting foot on my boat!"

"Captain," Joe quickly protested, "I've been waiting for years for someone to remake me— and Donald did it. He even had a . . . uh, brainstorm and gave me the right name! He's my new friend and . . . I want him to see a bit of

17

the world." Joe struggled to find the words to make his point. "Besides, the earthquake shook him up . . . as well as his house and his parents. Yup, I think . . . uh, some time away would do him good."

Captain Nimbo focused his eyes on Donald and shook his head from side to side. "I hate green sea boys, especially young ones with no brains yet. If he comes with us, Joe, you'll have to keep him out of the way. And if you don't, I'll stuff him in a filthy locker for the rest of the trip." With a scowl on his face the captain shook his pipe at Donald and gave him a warning. "That's an old box full of spiders, rats and lots of moldy stuff. You'll have to watch your step if you come aboard my boat, young man."

"Come on, Captain," Joe urged. "Shake hands. Donald's a great kid and I owe him a favor. If it hadn't been for him . . . well, I wouldn't be here."

"That's true," Captain Nimbo agreed, puffing on his pipe. "But *I* don't owe him any favors."

"Look here, Captain, he's got to come with us. Please, . . . uh, welcome him aboard," Joe insisted.

The captain gave a disgusted sigh and grumped, "Batten down your hatches, Joe. I'll shake his hand, but he'd better not get in my way or cause any problems."

Joe gently lifted Donald's small arm and the captain coldly took his hand, saying, "Well, come on then." Pointing to the ladder attached to the side of the boat, the captain stepped up, holding the lantern to light the way. Donald followed. They easily made their way to the deck, but the mudman moved more slowly.

"Get the anchor out of your pants, Joe, and get up here," the captain loudly ordered. The gigantic man wedged his big feet between the rungs of the ladder. He teetered from side to side, puffing and panting, as he climbed. Because he was so big and heavy, he was completely out of breath by the time he hauled himself on board.

Flipping on a dim light, Captain Nimbo remarked, "You're just a big old poop-out, Joe. And you've never been much of a rig climber." The mudman's huge shoulders fell and his head drooped. Noticing that his comments had dampened his friend's spirit, the captain added, "Hey, look, mate, I'm glad you're back! It's been a long time and I did miss you." Joe perked up, smiled his broad smile and gave the captain another hug—very gently this time.

Suddenly Joe 'Dobe tripped again. His bulky body sprawled on the deck of the boat. The captain jumped out of his way. "You bumbling bunch of ballast. Watch where you're going! You could destroy your body, my body and my ship." Irritated, Captain Nimbo shook his head and heaved a doubtful sigh.

Joe shrugged and gave Donald a friendly smile. "Yup, these big flat feet got in the way again," he said. "It bothers the captain a lot more than it bothers me. I'm clumsy . . . and I never did move as fast as he does, . . . but I've got a big heart in this muddy body of mine."

Captain Nimbo nodded in agreement, "That, he does. That, he does. I'm a mean, nasty guy, as you can probably tell. Most people won't come near me. Somehow, Joe found a way to like me and we've been good friends ever since."

The captain led them through the vast, almost empty lower level of the boat. Cars and trucks had once parked there during their ferry across the water. He guided them up the wide stairs to the passenger deck, which served as his living quarters. Glancing at Donald, the captain asked, "Joe, what are we going to do with this *second-greaser* while we get the ship ready to fly?"

"Turn on the lights and let him . . . inspect the boat," Joe suggested.

Captain Nimbo exploded with another fury of anger. "Let him loose aboard my ship? Never! I'd throw him over board hook, line and sinker before I'd let him have the run of this place."

"I won't touch anything. I'll stay out of the way. I know how to entertain myself," Donald quickly replied. He had always been interested in big machines and how they worked, so he was very eager to look around. Then the boy added, "Does this really fly?"

"Watch those questions, kid," Captain Nimbo said, blowing a foul cloud of smoke in Donald's direction. "You've got to know, I hate a bunch of stupid questions and I don't like nosy kids either."

Joe 'Dobe spoke up for Donald. "Lay off,

Captain. Just lay off. It's only a simple question. He's just curious."

Annoyed, Captain Nimbo answered, "Yeah, kid, this thing flies, but she hasn't been much of anywhere since Joe 'Dobe washed away. Why do you suppose I was so glad to see him? He's my first mate, my copilot, my friend! I hesitate to fly without his help. Lately, I've programmed a computer to be my copilot, but now that Joe's back, I'd rather have him beside me than a machine." The captain teased, "Besides, computers break down, Joe doesn't. He only falls down! Right, Joe?"

"Yup, that's right," Joe chuckled. Then he got a faraway look in his eyes and recalled, "You should see this ferryboat fly. It's a . . . miracle. Yup, she flies like . . ."

Captain Nimbo interrupted the mudman with a wave of his pipe and proudly explained, "She flies easy as a sea gull. I already had invented a super fuel that I named X-Pluto. I was sure it would give us the power we needed to get us off the ground. Some people didn't believe that my collapsing wings would work. They even called me a *crazy old salt*, but boy, did I fool them. After a few years I figured out the right combination to make her fly. I never could understand why Howard Hughes got more attention than I did."

Then Joe added mysteriously, "Donald, the captain hasn't told you everything. This old boat can do more . . . than just fly."

"Enough gibber-jabber. Time's a'wastin',"

the captain snapped, "so go ahead and look around the ship, Donald. But remember, I'll tie you to the anchor if you mess with anything."

"Okay, Captain. Yes, sir. I mean no, sir. I mean, I won't touch anything."

"And furthermore," the captain ordered, "when you hear the whistle blow, follow the sound up that staircase to the outside observation deck, then head up the smaller stairs to the pilot house." He pointed in the general direction. "That's where we'll be. Come on, Joe." They disappeared up a wide stairway at one end of the auto deck.

Donald was left alone to explore the boat. He decided to start on the top and work his way down. He ran up a broad staircase and found himself in a huge living room. There were several over-stuffed sofas, one gigantic leather chair and a wooden table with swivel seats on either side. An immense chair sat at one end of the long table. It was large enough to seat Joe 'Dobe. All the furniture was bolted to the hardwood floor. Walking around the room, Donald opened door after door and discovered several sleeping cabins with built-in beds and dressers. One was twice as big as the others, with a jumbo-sized bed. He could tell that it was Joe 'Dobe's room.

He poked his head into the galley, or ship's kitchen. It was a compact room with a high ceiling. There was an old-fashioned wood stove surrounded by huge pots, pans and platters. Once again, everything was tied down or enclosed in some way, especially the breakable dishes. He peeked into a deep pantry and could see that the captain had recently taken on supplies because the shelves were full of food.

Donald ventured downstairs to the auto deck. He felt like an ant as he explored the large space where the cars and trucks had once been parked for their cruise across the Bay. Small rooms full of inventions took up some of the parking area. He opened any unlocked doors and was amazed at the projects the captain was working on.

He walked straight ahead and peered over the front of the boat. He saw a mammoth iron hook hanging from the *bow*. "I wonder what that's for," Donald whispered to himself. He knew it wasn't an anchor. Turning around and looking up, the boy could see the captain and Joe standing in a tiny room two stories above. He figured he was looking at the pilot house.

Continuing his tour, he walked to the middle of the auto deck and opened a large double door. He went down the metal stairs into the engine compartments below. The engines were shut off, but the dark rooms were still hot because the motors hadn't cooled completely. The area was rather spooky, so after a quick glance at all the large pieces of machinery, Donald ran back up, his shoes clanging on the metal treads.

The next place he explored was the *stern*. Near the back of the boat he came to a large sealed cylinder and looked for a door knob. Instead, he found a small wheel. In his mind he could hear Captain Nimbo say "Don't touch that," but he turned it anyway. A panel of heavy metal siding slid open to reveal a deep pit. It looked like the inside of a large water well. Before he had time to investigate it, a shrill whistle blew, *wheeee*, and the captain called over the loudspeaker, "Ready for lift-off!"

Startled, Donald quickly turned the wheel to close the panel and ran up the wide flight of steps to the living quarters. He hurried up the narrower stairs to the top of the boat and felt a weak rumbling as he scrambled along the cramped walkway that led to a door marked PRIVATE.

By now the rumble had grown thunderous. The whole boat began vibrating, *rrrrmmmm, rrrrmmmm*. He heard the high screaming whine of a different engine, *eeeerg, eeeerg, eeeerg*. Donald covered his ears as the engine noise increased. He had trouble keeping his footing and was beginning to panic. He quickly opened the door and burst into the pilot house shrieking, "Joe, Joe. It's another earthquake!"

"Yup, it feels like an earthquake," the booming voice responded kindly, "but it's only on this boat."

"Oh, Joe. I'm scared!" Donald cried, trembling from head to toe. The mudman gently lifted him on to his large lap and put his big arm around the frightened boy.

With his right hand, Joe 'Dobe began pushing buttons and pulling knobs. By now his talking and thinking had improved and he explained, "We're testing the engines for take-off. That's why the boat is shaking. These engines are pretty powerful—they have to be to lift this boat from the ground."

"And don't you touch anything, kid," the captain ordered sternly.

Donald nodded, replying, "Yes, sir." Little by little he calmed down enough to look around. Windows surrounded them. Large windows were in the front and on the sides, giving them a good view of the area. Small, high windows were behind them, overlooking the smokestack and the top of the boat. Joe and the captain sat in two tall swivel chairs mounted to the right and left of the big pilot's wheel. A cushioned window seat, a large computer and a tiny desk were built into the back wall. Dials, switches and gauges filled the space below the front windows. Some of the equipment looked old, such as the compass sitting in an antique box with a glass lid. Some of it was high-tech, like the control panel of an airplane.

Captain Nimbo checked the gauges as the ferryboat rocked even more violently. "We're at full power, so fasten your seat belts and get ready for lift-off," he announced.

"Donald, would you like to push the LIFT-OFF button?" Joe asked.

"Wow! Yeah!!" Donald said, immediately forgetting his fears.

"Come on, Joe," Captain Nimbo interrupted, "he doesn't even know the ropes and you're asking him to be your *winger?*"

"Yup, Captain. That's right. I need a right-hand man. I'll show him what to do."

Captain Nimbo stomped his foot and puffed a storm cloud of smoke. "Just remember who's in command here. I'm the captain. You need to ask my permission or I'll hang you both by your thumbs from the flagpole!"

"Aye, aye, sir," Joe 'Dobe replied crisply. "Permission requested for Donald to push the LIFT-OFF button."

"Should a green landlubber who has to sit on your lap start the lift-off?" Captain Nimbo grouched, pulling his sea captain's hat down tightly. Then he added, puffing rapidly on his pipe, "Permission granted, but he's all yours to train, Joe. And make sure he doesn't mess up or get scared when you really need his help."

Donald felt both embarrassed and pleased as Joe 'Dobe gave him a quick hug of confidence. "Yup, Captain, this boy can do just about anything. You'll see," he promised.

Blowing a dense cloud of smoke from his pipe, Captain Nimbo asked, "Are you ready for lift-off?"

"Ready!" Joe 'Dobe confirmed. He reached over and pulled the cord that released a deep *boooomp* from the ferryboat horn. Tapping Donald lightly on the knee, Joe pointed at the LIFT-OFF button and directed, "Press that, Donald."

The boy followed Joe's instructions, being careful not to touch anything else on the instrument panel. Instantly the powerful jets kicked on and the ferryboat started to rumble and shake.

The crew began the final countdown.

10

9

8

7

6

5

4

3

2

1

LIFT-OFF !!

As they rocketed into the sky, Donald felt his body being forced by gravity into Joe's lap. The noise was deafening and the whole boat rattled as they left the ground, *pluu-uuuu-uuuu-uuuchhhhhh !!*

"She's up and away," Captain Nimbo cheered.

"Yup, we blasted off!" Joe hollered.

Wide-eyed, Donald exclaimed, "This is incredible. No one will ever believe it."

Suggested Activity: *Captain Nimbo uses many seagoing terms. What do you think these sea terms mean? Look in the dictionary or ask some of the sailors down by the wharf.*

Chapter 3

Into the Depths of the Bay

Captain Nimbo guided the ship straight up into the early morning sky. When they reached the proper altitude high above the mountains, he commanded, "Extend the wings, Joe."

"Roger, mate." Joe scanned the instrument panel to make sure he had the right button, then announced, "I'm turning us into an airplane." He pressed the button marked FLY and told Donald to look out the side window.

"Brace yourselves!" shouted Captain Nimbo. Immediately a strong jolt shook them. They bumped and rocked from side to side. Donald felt as if he was on a ride at the county fair, except this time he was far above the ground sitting in the lap of a mudman.

It was too dark for the boy to see the plastic panels telescoping from the sides of the boat. These formed transparent wings that converted the boat into a mammoth airplane. The aircraft shuddered as the pieces moved, connected and locked into position. When the ship was flying smoothly, Donald asked, "What does this boat look like now?"

"Don't worry my skull with a lot of stupid questions, kid," Captain Nimbo scowled, putting his pipe back in his mouth. "Can't you see I'm busy?"

"Captain, come on. Be nice to Donald," Joe gently scolded.

Chewing on his pipe and spitting out of the side of his mouth, the sea captain replied, "I already told him that I'm not nice and his questions bug me."

"Yup, I know. But Donald is just a young boy."

"That's the problem, Joe. I don't need a dingy *deck-monkey* hanging around this ship and asking me a lot of questions."

"How will he learn if he doesn't ask questions?"

"OK. OK, Joe. I'll answer him," the captain grumbled, as he created a haze of smoke with his pipe. Turning to Donald he added, "Just don't ask too many of them, kid."

Donald gulped and glanced at Joe. The friendly mudman winked at him to let him know that things would be okay. However, the boy knew that questions popped out of his mouth without his even thinking about it.

Pushing his sea captain's hat up on to his bushy hair, Captain Nimbo looked Donald straight in the eye. "So you want to know what this boat looks like now. Well, she looks strange. Very strange. Landlubbers think it's a Flying Ferry Boat because it's hard to see the clear wings from the ground. But she flies the same as a jumbo jet."

"Wow!" Donald commented, "I can't wait until the sun comes up so I can see."

Joe undid his seat belt, slid Donald from his lap and stood up. Looking out the window he inquired, "Are you heading to San Francisco now, Captain?"

"Yeah, to check out the earthquake damage and then to meet King Crab."

Remembering what the captain had said about asking questions, Donald gently poked Joe and whispered, "Who's King Crab?"

Joe whispered back in his ear, "Tell you later." Then he replied to the captain in his normal voice, "San Francisco. That's great. I want Donald to see the City and the Bay from up here." Smiling, Donald leaned his head on Joe's fat stomach and squeezed the mudman's big hand.

Captain Nimbo guided the Flying Ferry Boat northward and soon San Francisco Bay appeared below, vast and calm in the first morning light. The fog was gone and the wind was still. It was a crisp, cloudless November day. "We'll make a big circle and go all the way around the Bay while the sun is coming up," Captain Nimbo announced. "When there's enough light, we'll check out the destruction caused by the earthquake. There's not as much as you'd expect."

Joe pointed out the landing lights at the San Francisco airport on the west side of the Bay. In front of them, lights twinkled from hundreds of windows in the tall downtown skyscrapers, giving the City a magical appearance.

"Things have changed since you were last here, Joe," Captain Nimbo said, his pipe dangling from his mouth. "There are lots of new skyscrapers. I use that tall, triangular-shaped building to sight my bearings when I'm coming 'round."

In the pale pink light of dawn they spotted a tiny island straight ahead. "I've read about the prison on an island," Donald said. "Is that it?"

"That's Alcatraz, all right," Captain Nimbo responded. Then he went on to explain that it was no longer used as a prison, instead it was a popular tourist attraction.

Donald moved from window to window. "And is that the Golden Gate Bridge over there?"

Captain Nimbo grumped, "What am I, a tour guide? You mean you've never seen this famous bridge?"

"No, I haven't. We just moved here four weeks ago. But I've seen pictures of it."

"Well, stick with us, mate. You're going to see things that most people don't even know about," Joe 'Dobe chuckled.

"Like what?" Donald asked.

"Like the gate under the Golden Gate Bridge," Joe answered.

"What do you mean?" the boy questioned.

Joe patiently explained, "Just that—a gate, but it's made of real gold."

The captain added, "And it's hidden deep under the water beneath the Bridge."

Joe explained, "We close the solid gold gate when we pull the plug."

"Plug?! What plug?" Donald asked.

Captain Nimbo folded his hands across his chest and grunted, "I'm tired of all these questions. You answer the kid, Joe."

The mudman slowly gathered his thoughts. "Well, you see, there's a big plug right in the very deepest part of San Francisco Bay—about 350 feet down." Joe paused to point toward the location under the Golden Gate Bridge.

Not looking at the captain, Donald interrupted, "What's it for?"

Joe answered, "To let out the dirty water. You know how you clean the bathtub at your house? Well, we do the same thing here. We pull the plug in San Francisco Bay, scrub the dirty ring with King Crab's help and refill the Bay with clean water. It's probably been a long time since this has been done, right, Captain?"

Captain Nimbo nodded his head. "Yeah. The last time was when we did it together—and that was when I was a young man." The captain suddenly sat up straight and the scowl left his face. "Leaping dolphins, Joe, this would be a good time to swab the Bay! There's earthquake repair going on all over the City and everything's a mess anyway."

"Golly, Captain, I didn't bring Donald to work. I just wanted to get him away from home for a few days. I figured we'd fly around, take it easy and see what was going on in the Bay Area."

Donald jumped up and down asking, "Can we clean the Bay today? I'll help! How do we do it?"

Scowling again, Captain Nimbo put his hands over his ears, not wanting to hear any more questions. After a few minutes of silence and steady puffing on his pipe, the captain calmed down and muttered, "You see, Donald, three quarters of the Bay is less than 18 feet deep, so if we get most of the water out, it's pretty easy to clean. A crew of crabs helps us by nibbling the ugly green algae that covers the rocks along the shoreline."

"Can you still find the plug?" Joe 'Dobe asked.

"It should be easy with my Mebus 21. That's my new all-purpose computer."

Concerned that he might be replaced by a computer, Joe questioned, "Does it do the hookup, too?"

Donald's eyes opened wide with surprise and he blurted, "Hookup?! Is that what that big hook is for?"

"You ask more questions than a walrus looking for a sinking whale," Captain Nimbo complained, filling his side of the room with smoke.

Joe 'Dobe looked the captain in the eye before answering. "Yes, and controlling that big hook is my job. After the boat dives to the bottom, I hook the plug so we can pull it."

"Neat-o!" Donald replied, eager for more action.

All this time Captain Nimbo had been going north, following the shoreline. Now they were above San Pablo Bay, making a wide turn through the sky. The old seaman explained, "I installed the Mebus 21 because Joe wasn't here to help me. It's programmed to activate the gate, guide the ferryboat, find the plug and do the hookup, but I've never used it, so I don't know if everything actually works."

Turning to the captain, Joe asked, "Does the gate still go up and down?" But Captain Nimbo didn't answer. Joe reached over, tapped him on the shoulder and asked again, "Captain, does the gate still work?"

"You heavy-handed hunk of mud! Keep your hands to yourself." Captain Nimbo bristled beneath a growing cloud of smog.

"Well, does it?" Joe asked for the third time.

Ignoring the question, Captain Nimbo puffed another huge storm of smoke into the air and turned to fiddle with his computer. He swiveled back and forth in his chair, trying to fly the boat and operate the Mebus at the same time. Finally he mumbled, "It worked the last time we used it."

Joe shook his head, "But that was years ago, Captain."

Heaving a sigh, Captain Nimbo wished he was alone in the pilot house. It had been a long time since he had been visited by anyone. He didn't have many friends and was used to his quiet life. Having these two people ask him questions was driving him nuts, so he commanded, "Joe, fly these timbers. Take her the rest of the way around and then head south, toward Oakland. Just keep the water under the boat while I get some information from my Mebus 21."

Joe 'Dobe clumsily took over the controls of the Flying Ferry Boat and she began to rock back and forth. After all, it had been a long time since he had flown. He shifted his massive weight around in the big chair and struggled to keep the aircraft level.

"You goofy ball of mud! Fly right or jump ship," Captain Nimbo ordered.

Joe let out a sigh of relief when he got the flying boat under control, but Donald's stomach felt as if he had been on a roller-coaster. Captain Nimbo had turned his attention to the Mebus 21 and was typing in commands. A picture of the Golden Gate Bridge came on the screen, followed by a series of technical questions. The captain rapidly entered data into the computer until a large graph appeared on the screen. He blinked with disbelief. "This is incredible! The tide is right, the time is right and the weather conditions are perfect. It'll be several months before everything lines up like this again. I say let's go for it!"

"Go for what?" Joe asked.

"Go for pulling the plug," the captain said.

"Yes!" Donald exclaimed with a quick thumbs up gesture.

"What? Not yet! No way!" Joe immediately reacted. "It takes time to get things ready."

"Heavenly hardtack! Look here. Everything's perfect." Captain Nimbo could see that by the next morning the tides would be at their lowest point. That was important, because the plug sat in the deepest part of the Bay and there would be less water above it at a minus tide. When he looked at the weather forecast, it was clear and warm with no rain or fog predicted. "Why are you dragging your feet, Joe?"

Joe 'Dobe scratched his head and thought as hard as he could. His mind did not work nearly as fast as Captain Nimbo's and he wanted to be completely prepared before doing such a risky task. "Things can go wrong and I don't want Donald to be in danger."

Captain Nimbo took over the flying again and warned, "Don't forget, I am the captain and I command the people on board my boat."

Joe still protested. "But we've got to notify all the boat owners and get the ships anchored and find the plug and make sure the gate works and . . . whew, . . . I'm worried. You know there's a lot that can go wrong." Joe repeated, "Yup, a lot can go wrong."

Smoke poured from the captain's pipe and he sputtered an order. "*Heave to*, Joe. Get out your old checklist and quit your bellyaching! We're going to do it!"

Even though he still didn't agree, Joe followed orders and searched through the drawers of the tiny desk. He found a rumpled piece of paper listing a series of tasks: 1) Notify the Coast Guard. 2) Call the boat marinas and piers.   3) Call the newspapers.   4) Check the hook and the hook controller.

"There are some other things you need to do," the captain told him. "You'd better let the TV stations know.   I understand more people watch TV than read the newspapers.   And you need to call Donald's parents, too, so they won't think we've kidnapped their kid.   If they ask a lot of questions, tell them to watch the evening news." The captain handed Joe a card file. "The names and numbers are in here.   Tell everyone that the plug will be pulled at noon tomorrow."

With Donald's help, Joe began telephoning. Between calls, one more thought popped into Joe's head.   "Captain, are you sure King Crab will be able to help us?"

"Stop bugging me!   I'm certain there's no problem with the king.   He'll be glad to put those lazy little crabs to work cleaning their underwater home.   When we see him this afternoon, we'll tell him our plans.   Then it's up to him to warn the rest of the sea life to get out of the Bay."

"Will I get to meet King Crab?" the boy questioned.

"Trim those topsails and hold your tongue, kid!   Come on, Joe, you either shut this sea boy up or answer all his questions yourself." Captain Nimbo clamped his teeth on the stem of his pipe and turned his attention to flying the ship.

Donald whispered to Joe, "Wow, he sounds just like my parents."

Chuckling to himself, the mudman softly spoke to Donald, "Well, maybe when you learn how to work around the captain, it'll be easier to deal with your parents."

"Yeah, maybe so," Donald agreed.

"Now, you asked about King Crab. Yup, you'll meet him this afternoon. We'll be going to his grotto. He's the biggest crab you'll ever see."

Donald pressed his nose against the window. He wondered what a grotto was, what King Crab looked like and when all the excitement was going to start, but wisely decided to keep quiet.

Since the questions had stopped, Captain Nimbo relaxed a bit and began pointing out the sights. He showed them the oil tanks in Richmond, then dropped in altitude and followed the freeway to Oakland. The sun was bright as they cruised along. They saw where a huge section of freeway had collapsed when the giant earthquake came through. More than a mile of double-decked highway had been totally ruined.

Donald shuddered, "Oh, my gosh! Look at those smashed cars! Did anyone get hurt?"

"Yes, some died, but the fast action of the people who live in that neighborhood and the rescue workers saved many others who were trapped in their cars. Didn't you watch your TV?" Captain Nimbo asked.

"No, our house got wrecked and we didn't have any electricity."

Captain Nimbo stayed on course until he reached the southern end of the Bay. There he made a wide turn and headed toward San

Francisco again. He looked over the thin blanket of water and commented, "Just think mates, this will all be mud tomorrow night—almost 420 square miles of benthic mud."

Joe took a break from his telephone duties and began singing loudly—and off-key.

San Francisco here we come,
Right back where we started from!
San Francisco here we come,
Right back where we started from!
San Francisco here . . .

Captain Nimbo quickly put his hands over his ears and then commanded, "Knock it off, Joe. You know I can't stand your singing."

Disappointed, Joe quietly leaned back in his chair while the captain guided the flying ship past Candlestick Park. Soon they were directly over the Oakland-Bay Bridge. They could see the highway department working on the decking that had fallen during the earthquake.

The captain turned inland by the old Ferry Building and soared over Chinatown, pointing below. "Look, Donald, there's a cable car on that steep hill." They could see people hanging from the sides of the car as it climbed to the top. "And see that big, burned spot over by the boat marinas? When the earthquake hit, the ground down there changed into a muddy milk shake, and some houses crumbled. Then the gas lines broke and fires started."

"I bet those kids lost more toys than I did,"

Donald said.

Joe got a far away look in his eyes. "Remember me telling you about the 1906 quake, Captain? That was a real bad one. It burned most of the City."

"Yeah, your firsthand stories came to mind when this shaker hit."

"I sure don't like earthquakes," Donald said.

"Me neither," Captain Nimbo agreed.

Ignoring the captain's former complaint, Joe 'Dobe started singing again.

> *Yup, yup, yup.*
> *Golden Gate Bridge, here we are.*
> *Yup, yup, yup.*
> *In a boat, not a car.*

The captain started to cover his ears, but changed his mind and ordered, "Joe, you fly while I check out some things."

"Aye, aye, Captain."

Captain Nimbo knew the mudman couldn't sing and fly at the same time. Happy that it was quiet again in the pilot house, he turned to his computer. A dark, murky image had appeared on the screen.

Looking over the captain's shoulder, Donald remained quiet as long as he could, but finally whispered, "What's that?"

Captain Nimbo grumbled, "Your questions are just like ocean waves. They keep rolling in and no one can stop them." He chewed on his pipe for some time, but eventually answered the boy. "What you're looking at is the bottom of the Bay, where the real gate is located. This massive gold gate will rise on the east side of the Golden Gate Bridge until it forms a solid dam between the ocean and the Bay. When we pull the plug, it will hold the ocean water out until the crews of tiny crabs have done their job."

Puzzled, Donald eyes opened wide and he asked, "How come I haven't heard about this gold gate?"

"Look kid, this isn't another fish story. I'm not making this up," the captain remarked. "People have just forgotten all about it because the last time we used it was so long ago. Tomorrow you'll be able to see the slab of gold sticking above the water."

The captain ordered Joe to fly a few miles out to sea and then head back over the center of the Bridge. The mudman put the ferryboat into a curving turn. Following a flock of pelicans, they cruised over the blue water and circled the Farralon Islands before soaring smoothly back toward the City. While they flew, the captain sat hunched over the computer keyboard. He was typing in information and making notes on a large pad of paper.

"What's the computer telling you?" Joe asked.

Captain Nimbo leaned back in his chair and let some small rings of smoke gently rise from his pipe. "Everything's looking good. It's a go. We'll start closing the gate when we're directly over the Bridge. Get ready, Joe."

"Aye, aye, Captain." The Flying Ferry Boat

moved toward the narrow entrance to San Francisco Bay and slowly flew through the center span of the Golden Gate Bridge.

The vehicles on the Bridge had stopped moving, tying up traffic in both directions. People climbed out of their cars and were pointing at the Flying Ferry Boat. "Why is everybody staring at us?" Donald asked.

"We're some sight," Joe said, smiling broadly. "Yup, it's not every day you see a Flying Ferry Boat."

Captain Nimbo entered more data into his Mebus 21. "Stand by to activate the gate, Joe," he called, now puffing his pipe nervously. Under his breath he whispered to the computer, "Work, baby. Work."

"I'm ready, Captain," Joe reported.

"One . . . two . . . three. Go!" the captain barked.

Joe quickly raised a blue lever and locked it in place, then turned a large timer. "It usually takes 24 hours until the gate is completely closed. We'll pull the plug about noon tomorrow," he explained.

Donald had been moving from window to window, but now he looked intently at the computer. "Is the gate working?" the boy asked.

"Don't bother me, kid. Just look right here," the captain growled, tapping the screen and watching the Mebus 21.

After passing over the City, Joe 'Dobe landed the ferryboat with a huge *splaaaash* on the quiet waters near Candlestick Park. Donald was so busy concentrating on the computer monitor that he hadn't noticed their descent toward the Bay. Thrown off balance and frightened by the impact, the boy automatically reached for Joe's hand. "Was that another earthquake?"

"Nope, not this time. Look out the window," Joe said, giving Donald a brief hug. "We just landed on the water. Now hold on to the chair for a minute because I'm bringing in the wings. We'll be a regular old ferryboat in no time." The boat swayed from side to side as the wings slowly collapsed inside each other and disappeared into the hull of the ship. Donald was amazed to see them vanish so easily.

"Put on your sea legs, mates," said Captain Nimbo. "We're going to be sailors now."

Donald stood beside Joe 'Dobe, glancing from the computer to the Bay to his friend. He liked being with the mudman and was slowly getting used to the captain's personality. Joe squeezed the boy's hand. "Are you having a good time?" he asked.

"Yeah. This is great. What's next?" Donald immediately wanted to know.

"Hold your flounders, lad! Don't get ahead of yourself! I've got to take our bearings and check my instruments." Floating gently on the Bay, the captain quickly set to work doing calculations and checking his maps.

"Hey, watch right here on the computer." Captain Nimbo's finger traced a line across the screen. "Look at that. It's the sand moving on the bottom of the Bay." The old seaman was beside himself with joy. "That shows it's working! The gate is closing!" He smiled from ear to ear. Leaning back in his chair, he puffed on his pipe with satisfaction. Now that he knew the gate was operating properly, he let the Mebus 21 take over.

"I'm starved!" Joe announced abruptly.

"There's plenty of grub in the pantry," Captain Nimbo said.

Licking his lips, Joe 'Dobe asked, "Am I off duty then, Captain? Should I fix lunch for all of us?"

"Sure, mate."

Joe's fat stomach growled as he headed for the galley. "Are you two coming?"

"In a minute," the captain said. "First I have to turn this bag of timbers into a submarine and set the course for King Crab's grotto. The king needs to know we're pulling the plug."

Donald's eyes widened in surprise, "A submarine? Wow!"

Ignoring the boy's reaction, the captain moved to another set of levers and switches, and began pushing various buttons and knobs. "I've got to get the underwater gear in place. Hang on, we'll be bumping around again." They gripped their chairs while the ferryboat pitched and rolled. Outside the window Donald saw clear plastic panels appear one by one, overlap each other and hook together.

Captain Nimbo proudly laid his hand on the wall of the cockpit. "Kid, we'll soon be inside a big watertight bubble with a giant propeller in the back, my idea of a sub. What do you think of this invention?"

"It's super," Donald replied, smiling.

The captain almost smiled back, then went on to explain, "You know, you won't find this kind of equipment just anywhere. In the beginning this was a regular old ferryboat, but now it's a vessel that will transform three ways."

While the panels enclosed the big boat, the captain told Donald about buying it to transport cars, trucks and people across the Bay before the bridges were built. "In those days I was working long hours and wanted someone to help me. About then Joe appeared. He needed a job and a place to live. He was a big, strong worker and I had plenty of room, so I was happy to take him on board.

"One evening we were sitting on the deck watching the sea gulls and we began dreaming of flying. We decided to add wings to the ferryboat. I had already invented X-Pluto, a super powerful fuel that I figured would lift us off the ground. It took a long time to complete our unusual airplane. When we did, we could extend the wings and soar with the birds."

Donald felt like a real crew member as the captain talked to him. "How come you built a submarine?" he asked, swinging his legs from Joe's big chair.

"Well, the Bay needed cleaning and we had to have a submarine to pull the plug. With my ideas and Joe's strength, we built the acrylic bubble."

"What's *acrylic?*"

Captain Nimbo frowned, then answered, "It's a kind of plastic. You know, landlubbers said acrylic would never work. They sure missed the boat on that one. I used the same stuff on the wings. It's tough enough to do the job and easy to repair. Our plastic bubble is laced with grids of tiny wires and right now the Mebus 21 is checking the bubble for air leaks." Captain Nimbo pointed at the notice on the computer screen. "Dagnab, there's a little leak."

The captain pressed a red button on the control panel. This made the wire grid in the leak area heat up. Then the plastic melted and flowed into the hole, sealing it. While the acrylic was setting up, the seaman studied the computer screen. After a while, he performed another pressure test which let him know the leak was mended. Captain Nimbo announced confidently, "We're ready to dive."

Before he could reach for the controls, Donald blurted, "I pushed the LIFT-OFF button. Can I push the DIVE button, too?"

The captain hit his own forehead with the palm of his hand and replied, "Does a catfish meow? Can a shark do a jig? The answer is *no!* There's more to it than just pushing a button!" Donald's shoulders drooped and his chin fell to his chest. With an understanding glance, the captain changed his mind. "Well, . . . OK. Why not?"

Donald sat up straight and flashed him a big

smile. "Yes!"

"First, you need to sound the warning horn. Pull that," the captain said, pointing to a short rope with a big knot on the end. A loud horn blew—*hoooonk, hoooonk, hoooonk, hoooonk.*

"Now, pull down those two blue levers. That will fill the ballast tanks on either side of the boat with water, making us heavy enough to sink." Donald did as he was instructed and heard water pouring in somewhere far below.

Watching the dials on the instrument panel, Captain Nimbo put out his pipe. Drumming his fingers on the desk, he waited. It was some time before he gave the command, "OK, Donald, hit the DIVE button. We're headed for the bottom of the Bay."

Donald followed orders. A constant *rrrr, rrrr, rrrr* echoed in his ears as the noisy propeller steadily plunged them downward. Millions of tiny bubbles raced up the windows when they sank farther under the water. Donald had to open his mouth again and again to pop his ears. The sunlight gradually faded during their slide into the depths of the Bay. Soon Captain Nimbo flipped on the inside lights.

When they were near the bottom, the captain set the course for the grotto. The Mebus 21 took over, acting like an automatic pilot. Every 60 seconds it briefly flashed a picture of the rising gate on the screen. Everything was in order.

"We're on our way to King Crab's grotto. It'll take about half-an-hour to get there," Captain Nimbo said. "Let's go see what Joe's cooked up.

I'll bet you're hungry, huh, Donald?"

"Yeah, and I hope he's fixing peanut butter and jelly sandwiches for me."

The old captain and his new mate headed down the stairs together.

Suggested Activity: *Climb aboard the old white ferryboat located at the National Maritime Museum at the Hyde Street Pier near Fisherman's Wharf. Phone: 415-556-3002. Or ride a new ferryboat across the Bay to Sausalito or Tiburon Phone: 415-546-2628 for information. Phone: 415-546-2700 for reservations and tickets.*

Chapter 4

Collision Course

Banging on the thick galley door, Captain Nimbo hollered, "What's for lunch?"

"Stop! Stop where you are! I've got a *Joe 'Dobe Special* almost ready," the mudman bellowed.

The captain led Donald to a small sink to wash up. On the way he commented, "Joe won't let anyone near the galley while he's making his special. Secret ingredients, you know."

When they returned to the huge living area, Donald took another look around. The room was comfortably furnished like his family's den, except he did not see a television. At both ends there was a wide staircase that led down to the auto deck. The floors and walls were made of wood, so even though it was big, the room felt cozy.

The captain and Donald seated themselves in the swivel chairs on either side of the long dining room table. While they waited, wonderful smells came from the galley and they could hear their cook talking loudly to himself.

"Close your eyes, here it comes," Joe finally

called from behind the door. "Close 'em tight!"

They followed Joe's instructions, but Captain Nimbo was irritated. He folded his long arms across his flat stomach and grumbled, "Hurry up, Joe. I'm hungry and I don't want to play your silly games."

Joe kicked the swinging door open with his big foot and shuffled into the room.

Donald gulped and prepared for the worst. He whispered, "I only like peanut butter and jelly sandwiches."

"What kind of deck hand are you anyway?" the captain quietly replied. "You mean you're not going to try a *Joe 'Dobe Special*?"

Donald slouched in his chair and didn't answer. He listened to Joe stumble and plunk something on the table. "OK, you can look now," the big man said with childlike delight.

A six-foot-long sandwich, piled high with meat, cheese and vegetables of all kinds, filled the length of the table. Amazed, Donald sat up and stared at Joe's special creation. "Whoa! Where'd you get a loaf of bread like that?"

"Only San Franciscans make French bread like this," Captain Nimbo grinned. "When Joe let me know he was back, I called the bakery and they baked this one especially for him. I didn't forget, huh, Joe."

"Nope, you didn't. Thanks, I love this bread. How much sandwich can I cut for you, Donald?" Joe 'Dobe asked.

"I don't know. What's all that weird stuff inside?"

"You'll like it," Joe assured him.

Donald looked again. He hated vegetables and refused to eat them at home. "Just a slice. Maybe this much," he said, holding his finger and thumb about a quarter of an inch apart.

"Only that much? Don't worry, I'll finish what you can't eat!" The mudman cut a one-inch slice of sandwich for Donald. An eight-inch piece for the captain and took four feet for himself.

"Eat hearty, lad. There's a busy time ahead. Want a swig of coffee?" Captain Nimbo asked Donald.

"Coffee?" the boy questioned. No adult had ever asked him if he wanted a cup of coffee. "No, thank you. Do you have any cola?"

Joe nodded and disappeared into the galley. He returned with a can of soda and twelve big bottles of mineral water. Grinning at the thought of eating, he settled into his chair and began biting off enormous portions of the sandwich. He chewed with his mouth open, slopping food all over his lap as he helped himself to more. He didn't talk or even look around. Donald couldn't believe Joe's bad manners. If he had eaten like that at home, his parents would have sent him to his room.

The captain remarked, "When Joe eats, he eats. His brain shuts down when he's putting food in his mouth, but he'll be in fine shape once his stomach's full."

Donald finally took a tiny bite. He was prepared to spit it out, but instead he chewed

53

and swallowed. "Hey, this tastes OK." Somehow Joe's secret ingredients had made the veggies delicious.

Since the boat was on automatic pilot and the captain seemed more relaxed, Donald carefully inquired, "Captain, is now a good time to ask you some questions?"

"Just call me *Captain Encyclopedia*," the captain replied. "What do you want to know now?"

"Mainly, I want to know how you built all this stuff on the ferryboat."

"Don't refer to it as *stuff*. These are inventions, mate—machines, equipment, technology."

"How'd you figure it all out?"

"Things happen," Captain Nimbo shrugged. "You need this, you need that. I had a ferryboat and I wanted an airplane. I experimented with things a little bit every day. After all, building the tallest skyscraper or a rocket ship is only a matter of putting things together, one piece at a time."

"Did anything go wrong?"

"Well, sure. My first engine caught on fire. Later, my experimental wings collapsed. You may think this Flying Ferry Boat is a miracle, but she's not. Common sense, determination and hard work made this fancy ship. I asked lots of people lots of questions along the way."

"You did? Did they answer your questions?"

Captain Nimbo winked at Donald, "Not always. But like you, I kept asking, even when they got upset. How else do you get the information you need?" A glance of understanding flashed between Donald and the captain.

Joe 'Dobe finished off the sandwich and drank all twelve bottles of mineral water. He leaned his head back on the huge chair and soon was sleeping, snoring loudly. The captain turned toward the boy, "Hey, mate, you wash the dishes while I go to the pilot house to check my Mebus 21." Donald nodded and went to work carrying the dirty plates to the galley. Since he was part of the crew, he didn't complain about doing kitchen work.

The young boy was carefully wiping the big table when suddenly a tremendous crash smacked him flat on to the wooden floor, knocking the wind out of him. The lights flickered and the submarine became silent and dark, rocking back and forth.

Frightened and gasping for air, Donald cried out, "Joe, what happened? Where are you?"

Joe awakened abruptly from his deep sleep. "Uh, . . . still in my chair. I'm trying to stand up. Where are you?"

"I'm slipping and sliding all over the floor. The sub keeps tipping up and down." Donald's heart was pounding as he felt around in the darkness, trying to get his bearings. Suddenly a strange rumbling shook the boat. "Joe, what was that?!"

"I . . . I don't know."

After the racket stopped, the submarine tilted one last time and came to rest on an extremely steep slant, with the bow of the ship tipped down. Joe 'Dobe tumbled forward. His foot broke through the wood paneling, splintering the wall and trapping him. "Drat!" he bellowed. "My foot's caught."

At the same time Donald slid through the wide doorway and slammed into the backside of the narrow stairs. "Ooooch, that hurt," he wailed. "What's happening, Joe?"

"Golly, I don't know. Calm down and go find the captain. If I get my foot free, I'll come join you." As an afterthought, Joe pleaded, "And do be careful, Donald."

The boy bravely replied, "I'll try to get to the pilot house." He crawled around in the darkness. After a few moments, he touched the lower steps and felt a banister above him. Using it as a guide, he pulled himself up the tilted staircase.

When Donald reached the end of the railing, he knew the pilot house was somewhere directly in front of him. He crawled slowly along the tilted walkway until he felt the little steps. He stood up, balancing on the side of the tread, turned the door knob and pushed the door open. Peering into the blackness, he called, "Captain, where are you? Captain Nimbo? Are you OK?"

A faint *mmmmhh* was his answer. Donald tried to picture where everything was in the pilot house and where Captain Nimbo might have landed. Trying to keep from slipping on the steeply slanted floor, he felt his way into the room. Fortunately, his hand brushed a light switch and emergency lights came on throughout the boat.

"Hey, how'd you do that?" Joe yelled from below.

"I don't know," Donald called back. In the dim light he saw Captain Nimbo curled in a cramped space beside the wheel. He was lying absolutely still. The young boy crept to his side.

Joe 'Dobe poked his head into the small room and announced, "I'm here, Donald."

"Joe, the captain isn't moving. Is he dead?"

The mudman shook his head, hoping to think more clearly. "Who knows? Oh my, this is just what I was worried about." As he spoke, the strange rumble passed under them again. The ship vibrated and then all was still.

Joe cautiously moved his mammoth body into the small room, carefully balancing himself so he wouldn't slide into the instrument panel. He knelt beside his friend and touched the big lump on the captain's forehead. Then he gently shook him. "Come on, mate, wake up." Captain Nimbo only moaned.

Another rumble came from beneath them; then silence. "What is that?" Donald asked. "It sounds like a train."

Unable to work on such a steep angle, Joe decided to get the engines going and level the boat. He pushed the starter button, but nothing happened. He moved the throttle forward and tried again. The engine sputtered and quit. On the third try, the engine roared to life and the regular lights flashed on.

The mudman pulled back on the throttle, put the propeller in reverse, applied power and carefully leveled the submarine. He slowly guided her through the water and gently rested her on the bottom of the Bay. After he cut the power, he slumped in his chair, exhausted from thinking so hard. "I did it!" the big man shouted proudly.

Donald praised his big friend. "Good job, Joe."

Captain Nimbo was still curled up on the floor, but every now and then he would move slightly and groan. "I wish the captain would wake up," Donald said.

"Yup, we have to do something. Go get a wet cloth and some ice—and see if you can find a bottle of ammonia in the galley."

Donald left the little room and followed orders. When he returned, Joe gently placed the wet cloth full of ice on the captain's bump and passed the open bottle of ammonia under his nose.

Captain Nimbo's eyes fluttered opened. Brushing Joe's hand away, he sputtered, "Get that stinky stuff out of my face!"

"Captain, you've got to wake up!" Joe said.

"Blimey, my head hurts! Wh . . . wh . . . where the heck am I?" he asked, pulling away the ice pack.

"Relax, Captain, and keep that ice on your head," Joe directed.

"You got knocked out," Donald told him.

The captain looked around the pilot house with a blank stare. Then his eyes began to focus. "Yeah. Oh, yeah, I remember." He cradled his head and tried to explain what had happened. "I was hit by the boom when we were—no, that was another time. Let's see. Oh yeah, I was sitting at the computer and then suddenly I was flying through the air. I thought, 'Oh, cat's paw, we've hit a blinder.' But there's no reef in the Bay. That's the last thing I remember—oooh, oooh." The captain closed his eyes, rubbed his head and moaned again.

Joe gently patted his friend's shoulder. "Take it easy, mate," he soothed.

Another tremble came from beneath them. "There's that train sound again," Donald noticed.

"Yup, it keeps coming every so often," Joe commented.

Captain Nimbo sat up. "Blast it all! It's BART! That's the fast commuter train that travels under the Bay. How could I forget to program the location of the BART tube into my computer? We were on automatic pilot, you know, and suddenly—wham! We must have hit the bottom of our boat on the tube! Now we're sitting in Davy Jones' locker, 135 feet under the Bay."

Struggling to stand, the captain rubbed his head, "Spinning spinnakers, my head hurts. Get me a couple of aspirins, would you, kid? I feel like I've been kissed by a tugboat."

Donald ran downstairs to get the bottle of

aspirin. As he stepped off the last stair, he found himself ankle deep in water. "Oh, no," he cried. He quickly grabbed the bottle of pills and a glass of water from the galley. Racing up the steps, the boy screamed, "Help, help! There's water all over the floor. Captain Nimbo, it's flooded down there! We're sinking!!"

Suggested Activity: *Ride BART to the Merritt Street Station in Oakland. You can catch it underground along Market Street in downtown San Francisco. What is its route under the Bay? How far under the water is the tube? Where is the control center? Phone: 415-992-2278.*

Chapter 5

His Majesty, King Crab

Captain Nimbo rubbed the big bump on his head and grumbled, "Donald, ease your sails, will you? We're not sinking. We've already sunk and we're sitting on the bottom of the Bay. We've got a leak and I won't be swamped by a mere leak!" Then he quickly ordered, "Joe, fire up the bilge pumps and get that water out."

"Aye, aye, Captain," Joe replied, hastily going to work at the controls. The big pumps kicked in with a steady *raaaah, raaaah, raaaah,* rapidly draining the water from the lower decks.

Scared, but curious, Donald asked, "Captain, can you fix a leak while we're underwater?"

"I've never done it before, but there's a 50 percent chance that it'll work. Of course, that means there's also a 50 percent chance that it won't work." The captain touched his head and muttered, "Where's that aspirin, anyhow? My head hurts like crazy!"

Donald handed him the white pills and a small glass of water. Captain Nimbo swallowed the aspirin and turned to face his Mebus 21. He immediately barked, "Jib of jibs! Where'd the picture go? My computer's not working and I need it to fix the leak!"

Joe scratched his head, nodding, "I'm worried now. Yup, it's time to worry."

"How can you find out where the damage is without your Mebus?" Donald asked.

"That's just it, I'm at a standstill. I can't do a thing. Where's my pipe?" Captain Nimbo picked it up from the floor, carefully lit it and leaned back in his chair to think about the problems they faced.

While the captain smoked his pipe, Donald looked around the desk area. He spent some time checking the electrical cords and plugs like he had seen his dad do when their TV screen went blank. When he found a loose plug, he pushed it back into the socket. The computer immediately beeped and flashed back on.

"Well, what do you know, the deck-monkey fixed it. You're a smart shark, kid! That plug must have come loose when we hit the tube." Setting his pipe aside, Captain Nimbo quickly selected the program that would display the wire grids. Then he typed in the commands for the Mebus 21 to find the leak. The computer began its search and soon the captain knew the location of the damage. There was a hole in a panel under the bow of the boat, probably right where they had scraped the BART tube. He pushed a red button to begin the repair and heat was automatically applied to the wire grid around the leak.

"Cross your fingers, mates," he commanded,

hoping the water wouldn't cool the plastic too rapidly.

Joe looked at Donald uneasily. "Yup, cross as many fingers as you can."

"How's this, Captain?" Donald asked, showing him two crossed fingers on each hand.

Captain Nimbo didn't answer. He only raised his eyebrows and studied the computer screen. It was quite a while before he said, "By jingo, look at that. The acrylic sealed the leak."

Donald gave a whoop. "All right, Captain Nimbo!"

The captain heaved a sigh of relief and acknowledged him with a quick smile. "We won't have to surface after all, mates. We're seaworthy again!" Then he switched programs to take a look at the closing gate. "Jumping jellyfish! Look how much the gate has moved. That bump on my head has twisted my topmast and I'm not thinking clearly. Too many things are happening at once. I need to contact King Crab. And what about the boats in the Bay? Did you finish your calls, Joe?"

"Uh, . . . boats? Whoops, I got sidetracked by the crash," Joe confessed, pulling out his checklist. He quickly picked up the phone and began punching in the numbers that Donald helped him find. He repeated the same information over and over. *Anchor all boats securely or leave the Bay by midnight. The plug will be pulled at noon tomorrow to drain the water from the Bay.*

Captain Nimbo was studying the computer screen when Joe noticed a bright blue light flashing on the control panel. "King Crab's here! He found us!" the mudman declared.

The injured sea captain lightly massaged the bump on his head. "Oh, blubber! Not something more to deal with?! But, I do need to talk to him. As first in command, it's my duty to welcome him aboard. Come with me, Donald. You've been wanting to meet King Crab."

They left Joe 'Dobe talking on the telephone and walked carefully down the wet stairs to the auto deck. The bilge pumps had drained most of the water, but there were still puddles on the floor and drips coming from the ceiling.

The captain led Donald to the large cylinder-shaped room the boy had seen earlier. He opened a control panel hidden in the wall. Red lights were blinking. "This means King Crab has already opened the outer door and is inside the water lock," the experienced seaman explained. Another flashing light indicated that the room was sealed. When a group of orange lights flashed, the captain threw a switch. "I'm pumping out the water now." They listened to the water gurgling inside the circular room. Finally the captain ordered, "Donald, turn the wheel to open the door." Excited, the boy twisted the familiar wheel and the huge metal panel slid open.

A massive pink-orange crab filled the entire tank. Legs moved everywhere. Donald's eyes widened. His mouth fell open and he could only stare at the enormous crab who wore a glittering crown on his head, a black bow tie around his fat neck and a sparkling ring on one claw.

Being polite for a change, Captain Nimbo said, "Welcome aboard, Your Majesty."

Irritated, the king responded, "Save your greetings until I get out of here, would you?"

The captain ordered, "Well, shake a leg and get your body on deck."

"Can't you see?" the king replied. "I'm stuck in here. I must have grown since I last used this entrance."

"What do you want me to do about it?"

King Crab commanded, "Captain, get me out of here at once!"

"Pipe down, King. Come here, Donald. Help me. Grab any part of him and pull," the captain said.

Donald hesitated. He didn't know what or where to grab. King Crab's claws were moving in every direction. His main pincers opened and closed like giant jaws. His other legs had sharp looking barbs on them and gooey, green moss hung from his body.

The two of them tried to free the enormous crab. Donald briefly tugged on a back claw, but one of the giant pincers caught his sweat shirt and lifted him off the ground, shaking him back and forth. "HELP!! Put me down! Let me loose!" the boy screamed. The surprised crab quickly released him.

"What's that pestering me?" King Crab snapped.

"A little landlubber," laughed Captain Nimbo. "He's Joe 'Dobe's friend."

65

"Joe 'Dobe? Is he back?" the king asked. "Go get him! He'll get me out of here."

Captain Nimbo tried to calm him. "Settle down, King. I can hear Joe coming now. We'll get you out, but we might have to use some *soogee moogee* to do it."

King Crab immediately disagreed. "I hate sailor's magic, so forget it!"

When Joe 'Dobe arrived, he took one look at the big crab and his whole belly began to shake with laughter, "Looks like you're in a bit of a pickle."

"Show me some respect, you big clod of mud. I know a lot of sand has shifted since I last saw you, but I'm still the king. See this crown on my head? And this ring on my claw? All the sea life bows down to me!"

"Nobody would bow to a big can of crab meat," Captain Nimbo joked deliberately. "Live crab meat, fresh in the can! I could charge tourists to come take a peek at you."

"Quit teasing me, you dimwit. Get me out of here!" King Crab raged.

"Your Majesty," Joe said kindly, "stop your wiggling and give me a claw." He grabbed the upper part of a large flopping leg. Keeping clear of the main pincer, he pulled with all his strength. Suddenly . . . POP!! Joe fell backwards. He hit the deck and split a few planks where he landed.

"Yipes!" King Crab yelled.

"There you go, King!" Joe 'Dobe announced proudly. "I got you out."

King Crab fumed, "There I go all right! You

big oaf, you just broke off my leg and I'm still stuck in here."

Sprawled on the floor, Joe glanced at the huge leg in his hands and then back at the tank full of crab. "Oh, no! I'm sorry," he cried.

King Crab was not pleased. "I was going to give you a crab leg for dinner, but it appears you've already helped yourself. Now get on your feet and pull me out!"

Joe tossed the big leg aside, struggled to stand and stumbled across the deck to try again. He and the captain each grabbed an edge of the king's shell, turning him sideways. Together, they maneuvered him back and forth, while Donald guided the first three legs through the opening. Then they squeezed his body through the doorway, bringing along the remaining four legs.

King Crab shook out the kinks and breathed a sigh. "I don't want to get stuck like that again, so you'd better make a bigger door if you expect me to come on board this boat." He adjusted his crown, straightened his bow tie and stood up regally, declaring at last, "I do thank you for getting me out, gentlemen."

Captain Nimbo removed his hat and bowed slightly, "I welcome you aboard, King." Donald removed his cap and bowed as the captain had done.

Joe gave the shell a friendly pat, shook the big claw with the ring on it and said, "Hello, Your Majesty. It's been a long time."

"Where have you been, Joe 'Dobe?"

"Well, I took a lengthy mud bath and now I'm back. How have things been under the Bay, King?"

"Let me think. There have been a few oil spills here and there. Of course the BART tube was quite an intrusion on my territory. We had a celebrated visit by that famous ship *Queen Elizabeth II*. There was a lot of excitement when Humphrey the Whale came to visit me. And the earthquake made us rock and roll a bit. But, life goes on under the Bay." King Crab rambled on until he noticed Donald staring at him. "And who are you?"

The boy politely answered, "I'm Donald Jordan, Your Majesty."

"Donald's the kid who rebuilt Joe," Captain Nimbo explained. "It was Joe's idea for him to come on the ferryboat with us."

Extending his claw to shake Donald's hand, King Crab replied, "I'm pleased to meet you."

"I'm pleased to meet you, too. Does your leg still hurt?"

"Which one? I've got seven." The giant crab waved his remaining legs.

"The one Joe 'Dobe pulled off," the curious boy answered.

"That little one? No. It hurt when Joe yanked it off, but only for a second. Besides, it will grow back eventually. My legs are like a lizard's tail, when one breaks off, another one grows. It's handy when I need to escape quickly, and my enemy gets a delicious meal for his hunting efforts. In the meantime, . . ."

68

Captain Nimbo interrupted the conversation, "Sorry, King, I know how much you like to talk, but we must get down to business here."

With a shrug of his shell, King Crab gave in. "Okay. Business first, but then let's go to my palace."

"Visiting with you while the gate is closing has always been our tradition," the captain agreed.

"Hold it right there!" King Crab was suddenly irate. "What do you mean, 'while the gate is closing'? Are you saying that you started closing the gate without even asking me?"

"Yes, King, I am. I'm the captain and the time was right. Everything was perfect—the tide, the weather, everything. In fact, we're pulling the plug at noon tomorrow and you need to know the plans."

"But you didn't ask me. I'm the king. I'm the one who decides when the Bay gets cleaned."

"I'm the captain and I control the gate. It's up to you to tell the sea life to leave the Bay. And the gate is already closing."

With a twinkle in his eye, Joe turned to Donald and chuckled, "These two are still at it. I would have thought they could have decided who was in control by now. But nope, they continue to quarrel. It's difficult to say who's in charge when you have a king and a captain."

"You need to ask my permission next time, Captain," the crab demanded.

"If there is a next time," the captain warned.

Joe 'Dobe stepped in to referee. "Okay, you

two, simmer down."

"I don't want any of his subjects being washed down the drain," Captain Nimbo pointed out.

"Just you let me take care of that," King Crab snapped. "I'll send out my messenger crabs as soon as we get to the grotto. It will be a very clear message. *King Crab wishes to inform you that Captain Nimbo is pulling the plug. Leave the Bay by midnight or you will die.*"

"I hope those young fish and crabs heed your warning this time, King," Captain Nimbo declared. Then he turned to Donald and explained, "You see, information can travel like a storm if each crab or fish passes the news properly. It works fine until one fish fails to tell the next fish. A lot of the young ones don't know what happens when the plug is pulled. The last time was so long ago." The captain turned and questioned the big crab, "Do you remember the rest of your duties, King?"

King Crab nodded regally. "Of course I do," he sniffed. "After I make sure the sea life has left the Bay, I locate the plug for you. Then I organize the scavenger crabs to clean the entire shoreline. On land they would call this a no-sweat job."

Annoyed by King Crab's superiority, Captain Nimbo turned away from him and asked, "Joe, how are you doing on your checklist?"

"Donald and I have called everyone, but we still need to inspect the hook," Joe answered.

"Then let's go over the plans one more time," Captain Nimbo said.

King Crab became impatient. "I've had enough of your planning, Captain. Remember, we always go to my grotto while the gate is closing."

"I said we would do that, King. It's been our tradition. Just don't forget we have a lot of work ahead of us, so we can't stay too long." Captain Nimbo headed to the pilot house, revved up the engines and set the course for the underwater entrance to King Crab's home.

The king boasted, "Now you get to see where I live, Donald."

The boy was instantly curious. "Where is your palace?"

"That's top secret information. If I told you, you might tell someone else and soon it would become a tourist trap."

"I was only wondering," Donald commented.

"By the way," King Crab warned, "it's cold and damp where I live. You'd better bring something warmer to wear."

"There's a slop chest in my cabin. You'll find some warm clothes in it," Joe offered.

Donald turned to go upstairs, but the detached crab leg blocked his way. "What about this?" he asked, walking around it.

"That's our dinner. Yup, we'll carry it to Fisherman's Wharf and cook it in the big crab pots," Joe answered. "We'll eat cracked crab, San Francisco French bread and a green salad from Alioto's restaurant for dinner. Yum! I can hardly wait."

Donald's stomach churned and he made a

face as he thought about eating the mossy leg. King Crab noticed his turned-up nose. "What's the matter, Donald? Don't you like crab legs?"

Donald smiled weakly. "I like peanut butter and jelly sandwiches—and I usually don't eat people's legs."

"Well, I'm not a person, even though I am a king. But I don't blame you a bit," King Crab said with understanding. "And don't worry, I won't eat your leg, if that's concerning you."

By now the overwhelming fishy smell of King Crab was making Donald sick to his stomach and he was glad to have a reason to go upstairs. "See you later, Your Majesty," Donald said, leaving the enormous crab with Joe on the lower deck. The boy hurried to his mud friend's cabin and quickly selected a well-worn sailor's coat from the pile of clothes in the old trunk. Trying it on, he checked out his reflection in the bathroom mirror and was pleased to see that he looked like a sailor. Now he was definitely ready to visit the palace.

Donald joined Captain Nimbo in the pilot house and watched as the submarine chugged steadily ahead, *rrrr, rrrr, rrrr.* The boy saw several large fish and a sea lion pass in front of the big windows. The crew moved through the dimly lit water for a long time, then suddenly they were in the dark. The captain informed Donald, "We've entered the underwater tunnel to the palace. We'll be surfacing very shortly." The excited boy squirmed in Joe's tall chair. He was bursting with curiosity.

The captain emptied the ballast tanks and the submarine gradually surfaced. Soon they were floating in total darkness inside the protected grotto. Captain Nimbo warned over the intercom, "Hang on to the masts, men. This sub is going to wobble around while I convert her into a ferryboat." He pressed a button and the plastic panels bumped, shifted and withdrew into the hull of the ship. Then he turned on a mast head light, gave the old white boat a bit of power and guided her across the calm water to the wooden dock. Pulling the cord, he gave a long blast on the big ferryboat horn to announce their arrival, *boooomp!*

As the noise echoed in the immense space, hundreds of little white lights came on in the rocks far above their heads. A moment later the huge cave was absolutely quiet, except for the tiny waves that lapped on the sand.

Suggested Activity: *Learn about San Francisco Bay by visiting the Bay Model Visitor Center, 2100 Bridgeway in Sausalito. Call ahead for the hours and to see if there is water in the model. Phone: 415-332-3870.*

Chapter 6

King Crab's Royal Palace

While Captain Nimbo docked the old boat, Donald stood on his tiptoes, peering through the window. "Oh, wow!" he exclaimed, "This grotto is really big. It must be the size of my school, including the playground."

"It's big, all right," agreed the captain, "although it seems smaller when the tide comes in and fills it with more water. Fortunately the palace rooms are all above the waterline. However, the path in and out of King Crab's home gets flooded, so we have to watch the tides carefully."

Captain Nimbo shut down the engines and checked the Mebus 21, which showed that the gate was closing on schedule. He left the pilot house with Donald tagging close behind. He went to his cabin, put on his big woolen jacket and slipped a flashlight into his pocket.

While they were walking downstairs, King Crab scuttled sideways past the railings and scurried away to his palace to prepare himself for their visit. Donald told the captain, "I wish I had a video camera. I'd like to show my parents this grotto. They just won't believe it."

"No, they probably won't," the captain agreed.

"Why did King Crab want us to come here?"

"Oh, he likes to show off his palace and tell stories to anyone who will listen. Also, he loves music and wants to play his new electronic keyboards for us," the captain answered as they joined Joe.

When they left the boat, the tide was slowly creeping up on the shore. Donald grabbed the mudman's hand and Captain Nimbo led them down the dock to the sandy path. Briny smells from the crabs who lived there filled their noses. The grotto would have been gloomy without the tiny lights that twinkled from the rocky ceiling and reflected in the deep water. The crew felt as if they were surrounded by dancing stars.

Donald gasped again and again, "Oh, wow! Gee, this is great!" He held tightly to Joe's large hand and whispered, "How did we get in here?"

"We went to the very bottom of the Bay and came in through a secret tunnel. That's the only way in at low tide."

Donald whispered again, "Where exactly are we?"

"More questions," Captain Nimbo sighed.

"Yes, sir, Captain. They just pop out of my mouth. How else would I get the information I need?" Donald responded, feeling somewhat bold in his sailor's coat.

The experienced seaman smiled faintly and answered Donald's question. "I'll tell you where we are. But just you remember, scurvy and ship's lice attack anyone who reveals this location. So beware!"

"I won't tell. I promise."

The captain turned to the boy and whispered in a low voice, "We're under Alcatraz. Crab kings have lived under here for centuries, continually improving and redecorating their grotto. The prisoners never knew about the valuable treasures stored beneath them. And even now no one knows that the area under 'The Rock' is hollow and contains a palace."

Donald let out a low whistle, then zipped his lips to hold in the secret. He let go of Joe's hand and walked with pride because he knew the captain had entrusted him with private information. They followed the path along the water, then took a series of turns through a maze of large boulders. Four young crabs guarding a hidden entrance abruptly stopped them. "Who are you and what is your business here?" one demanded.

"I'm Captain Nimbo and this is my crew, Joe 'Dobe and Donald Jordan. We've been invited here by the king." Captain Nimbo puffed on his pipe and Joe tapped his foot while one of the crabs went to get approval for them to go inside.

In time, the crab returned and directed the other three to roll away a huge stone, revealing the entrance to a smaller cave. The visitors waited there until a uniformed crab appeared. He led the guests to a splendid throne room and ushered them down a side aisle to the shell-shaped seats in the front row.

Another crab entered through a side door and turned on some floodlights. Every time they came to visit the grotto, Captain Nimbo and Joe 'Dobe were impressed with its beauty. Brilliant jewels and beautiful seashells covered the walls of the room. Pressed abalone shells formed the multicolored floor. Varieties of coral were arranged to look like house plants. Lights shined on the chests of treasure that sat around the edge of the chamber. Donald stared at the priceless collection.

Soon a trumpeter blew on a pink conch shell to announce the entrance of the king. King Crab strutted grandly down the center aisle. He wore an emerald green seaweed cape and a fancy crown embedded with colored jewels. Several small crabs followed and helped him get settled on his ornate golden throne.

"I welcome you all to my palace," King Crab said proudly. "Captain Nimbo, it's good to have you as my guest. Mr. 'Dobe, I'm certainly glad to see you again. And Donald, your being here makes this visit extra special for me." Captain Nimbo and Joe 'Dobe guided Donald to the throne. They bowed to the underwater king and kissed the sparkling ring on his extended claw. No longer afraid, Donald also gave the royal pincer a loving squeeze. "Donald, since this is your first time here, I would like to offer you a gift to remember this day." King Crab smiled broadly and generously motioned toward the piles of treasure.

"Wow! You really mean it?!" Wide-eyed, the

boy scanned the ancient chests full of gold coins and valuable jewels, wishing he could have one of each. He thoughtfully selected an antique gold coin and buried it deep in his pocket so he wouldn't lose it. "Thank you, King Crab. I'll keep it forever," Donald said. "Where did you get all this treasure?"

"Shipwrecks, hundreds of shipwrecks. Also, nobility from other ocean kingdoms bring offerings to me at our midsummer's celebration."

Donald exclaimed, "You must have millions of dollars just sitting around in here!"

King Crab smiled and replied, "I don't use money like people do. This treasure has a different value to underwater creatures. The value to me is its beauty. I love to hold the stones to the light and see the reflections against the grotto walls. I stack the coins to make beautiful designs and I jingle them to create music."

"King," Captain Nimbo interrupted, "we need to get back to business."

"Pardon me, Captain, but I was trying to educate the boy by taking time to explain our ways under the Bay."

"I heard you, King," the seaman snapped. "Just remember, the gate is closing and your subjects have to get out."

"OK, OK!" King Crab grumbled. He rapidly clicked his giant pincers and six medium-sized crabs entered the chamber from the side door.

"Yes, Your Majesty," they said in unison, bowing low.

"An urgent message needs to go out to all of my subjects. Everyone must leave the Bay immediately because Captain Nimbo is pulling the plug at noon tomorrow."

"Will they all get out by then?" the captain asked.

"I'm not sure," one of the guards answered. "Many of the younger fish are afraid to go outside the gate. They think the waters of the upper Bay are safer than the ocean."

"They'll die!" King Crab exploded. "You tell them to leave before it's too late. I don't want any of my subjects swirling down in that whirlpool of water and disappearing into the nothingness below the drain. This is the message you must give them: *Captain Nimbo is pulling the plug. King Crab orders all sea life to get out of the Bay by midnight or you will die!!* Go pass the message. Now!" The crabs bowed to their king and hurried away to carry out his command.

King Crab shook his head sorrowfully, "This younger generation. They only want to do things their own way. They don't pay attention to history. What will they do when they inherit the sea?"

Captain Nimbo consoled him. "King Crab, you can only do your best. You've sent out the warning, now it's up to them to obey."

"Yes, I know that, but I still worry. However, it's out of my claws now," King Crab said.

"Yup, that's right," Joe agreed.

Setting his worries aside, the crab commanded, "Now, we must have our traditional visit. Remember, that means I talk and you listen! My stories will be new to Donald and I'm sure he'll want to hear them all."

Captain Nimbo leaned back, getting as comfortable as he could on the smooth shell. He knew he was stuck for a while listening to King Crab's same old long-winded yarns.

The royal crab spoke to his captive audience. "You're probably wondering about me, Donald, so I'll tell you. I have ruled this underwater kingdom for many years now. My father reigned before me and his father before him. When my father was king, people were moving to San Francisco because of the Gold Rush. Unfortunately they polluted the land and the water. Fish, clams, crabs, seals—all the sea life—had to live in the dirty water. As a young crab I heard stories of how this Bay used to sparkle. I dreamed of being the one to restore it to its natural beauty.

"Shortly after I became king, I met Captain Nimbo. As you can tell, he's quite an inventor and problem-solver. I told him that during the Gold Rush some miners had built a golden gate deep beneath the water at the narrow entrance to the Bay. It went up and down using ropes and pulleys and I heard it kept the gold from washing out to sea when the rivers were flooding. I also told him about the location of a gigantic plug in the deepest part of the Bay. My theory was if you pulled this plug, it might drain the dirty water.

"I asked the captain if he had any ideas. Of course he did—he'd use his boat. He went right to work figuring out how to make his ferryboat dive and invented a hook mechanism to grab on to the plug. He also needed a real good propellant that would give him lots of quick power and pull a huge amount of weight. That was when he invented X-Pluto. Finally he made the miners' gate work with a push of a button, so it was easy to open and close. May I point out that this all happened long before the Golden Gate Bridge was built."

King Crab continued, "About the time the submarine was ready, Joe appeared. The captain realized he needed a strong person to operate the hook, so he invited Joe to come on board. That's how it all started and ever since then the three of us have worked together to clean the Bay. By the way, did you know there were legends about Joe 'Dobe?"

"Really? Will you tell them to me?" Donald requested.

Already restless, Captain Nimbo whispered in Joe's ear, "Aren't those tales worn out by now?"

Speaking in a louder voice to get Captain Nimbo's attention, King Crab ordered, "Captain, no whispering while I'm talking. We tell these tales to our crab and fish children and Donald should hear them too."

The two glared at each other for a minute before Captain Nimbo shrugged his shoulders and King Crab spoke again. "You see, Donald, long ago San Francisco was a much smaller city and everyone on the docks knew Joe 'Dobe. They also knew that once or twice a week he ate stuffed goose for his supper and it took several to satisfy his big appetite.

"When Joe 'Dobe plucked his fat, tender geese, hundreds of fluffy under-feathers drifted away with the evening breeze. This light goose down made a milky-white fog that would blanket San Francisco as the sun was setting. Looking up, people back then would say, *Joe 'Dobe must be having a goose dinner again. Look at all those feathers floating across the sky.*"

King Crab paused for a response from the boy. Donald only looked puzzled, so the king explained, "You see, it really wasn't feathers at all. It was just the fog coming in."

Donald thought for a moment, then responded, "Oh, I get it. Will you tell me another one, Your Majesty?"

Captain Nimbo rolled his eyes. "Don't encourage him, kid."

King Crab let the captain's comment slide right off his shell and started another story. "Joe 'Dobe's house had a cellar under it like many of the older homes did. He stored canned goods, apples, onions and potatoes down there. One year while Joe was out in his garden digging up his potatoes, he felt a terrible storm blowing in from the ocean. You know Joe can't get wet, so he was in a big hurry to get the potatoes into the cellar before it began to rain.

83

Instead of putting them in mesh bags and storing them properly, he hastily dumped basketful after basketful down the wooden cellar steps. They made a terrific noise as they tumbled. *Thuuuud, boooom, boooom, ruuuumble, ruuuumble!* The loud bumping noise echoed throughout the neighborhood. Today, when thunder rumbles, we tell our children not to worry. It's probably Joe 'Dobe rolling potatoes down into his cellar!"

"I like that one. Our house in Kansas had a cellar. We even kept potatoes down there, so I know what you're talking about this time," Donald said. He sat forward on the bench and waited for the next story.

Captain Nimbo kept his mouth shut as King Crab began, "Every evening Joe 'Dobe took his dog for a walk in Golden Gate Park. In those days there were no leash laws so his dog was free to wander. One night, it was extremely dark, with no moon at all. While walking along the path, his pet spotted a squirrel. The little dog chased after it and soon disappeared in the bushes. Joe called and whistled, but his dog didn't come, so he ran home to get his enormous flashlight. When he returned to the park, he shined the bright beam of the flashlight everywhere searching for his lost pet.

"Night after night Joe went back to the park. His big light flickered like a searchlight through the sky, but no matter how hard he tried, he couldn't find his pup. People who lived nearby noticed the beam moving through the sky, flashing first one place then another. Today, when lightning bolts over the Bay, the younger sea life remember what their parents told them— that it's no doubt Joe 'Dobe with his big flash- light, out searching for his lost dog."

"Did you ever find him, Joe?" Donald asked.

"Nope. He completely vanished that night."

Captain Nimbo grew impatient during the story-telling. He stretched and threw his shoul- ders back, saying, "Hey, Your Highness, is story hour almost finished?"

"Yes, Your Rudeness, I'm done," crabbed the king.

Donald defended him. "I liked the stories. Whenever I see fog or lightning or hear thunder, I'll remember what you told me here in your grotto. Thank you, King Crab!"

"You're very welcome. I'm glad you brought Donald along, Joe. He shows me a lot of respect." Raising an eyebrow, the king looked at Captain Nimbo and commented, "That boy knows how to be a gentleman."

"So what?!" the irritated captain barked. "It's time for us to get out of here. I'm worried about the tide."

"Not yet. I must play some music before you leave," King Crab insisted.

"Do you really have a set of electronic key- boards?" Donald asked.

"That I do." King Crab pushed himself from his throne and tiptoed sideways towards a broad doorway.

Captain Nimbo repeated, "We really do have

to go now. The tide is getting higher every minute."

"Ignore the captain. He's always in such a rush to get going. Please come this way into the concert hall, my friends." They followed the king into a domed theater with smoothly polished stone walls. King Crab pointed at the front row and said, "Have a seat while I get into my costume."

The big crab disappeared behind a curtain of thin shells, leaving his guests to select seats on the padded rocks that rested in a semicircle. In a short time, the lights dimmed and the curtain opened to reveal the king dressed in a custom-made tuxedo that was covered with gold sequins. One empty sleeve flapped at his side. Around his barely visible neck, he now wore a twinkling bow tie. He looked dazzling.

"I will now perform the seven-claw version of the *1812 Overture*," he announced, flipping his coattails. The room exploded with music as King Crab attacked his keyboards. He twisted and swayed using five of his claws to operate the keys. The remaining two worked the pedals and other controls.

Donald covered his ears to muffle the noisy symphony as it echoed off the rock walls of the small cave. Joe 'Dobe happily rocked back and forth with his eyes closed. King Crab was in his glory, but Captain Nimbo wriggled impatiently. When the final cannons boomed and the chimes played, the whole grotto shook. Suddenly the lights went out and the music abruptly stopped, leaving them in pitch black silence.

Captain Nimbo leaped into action and yanked his flashlight out of his coat pocket. He turned it on, but nothing happened. He guessed the batteries were dead. Upset, he sputtered, "Now you've done it, King. Look lively there and get your lights back on."

"Oh, pshaw, I can't. I've blown the main power supply," King Crab muttered. "When it blows, it blows. I've done this before. I knew I'd wreck the electrical system if I turned everything on at once. The problem is when I start playing this great music, I totally forget everything else."

"You sea gull brain! You shell-head!!" Captain Nimbo swore. "When will you learn to follow directions? You can't order electricity around like you can a bunch of fish."

"Nimbo," King Crab cautioned, "I resent those remarks."

"Well, I resent being in the dark. I can't see a blasted thing!"

"Then why didn't you bring a flashlight that works?" the crab king said, giving the captain a bad time. "Let me remind you, crabs can see in the dark. If you'll just follow me, I'll lead you out. I do know my way around."

"Hold on a second, King. What does it take to get your power source functioning?" Captain Nimbo asked, still shaking his flashlight.

"I need new parts from San Francisco."

"Then get us back to the ferryboat, oh great leader!" the captain ordered.

87

While the king and the captain insulted each other, Donald moved closer to Joe 'Dobe and reached for the comfort of his strong hand, whining, "I don't like the dark."

"Nope, neither do I," Joe complained. "And if the tide is in, I'm in big trouble. Yup, if any part of my mud body touches the water and gets wet, it'll wash away. I've got to see where I'm going."

"Quit your bellyaching, Joe," Captain Nimbo grumbled, still fidgeting with his flashlight.

"I'm scared," Donald wailed.

"Pipe down kid, and forget the scared stuff," the captain scowled. "Right now we've got to get out of here."

King Crab broke into the conversation. "Hold on to one of my legs, Nimbo. You come next, Donald, and lead Joe. And if you touch any water, warn him immediately."

"OK, I'll try," Donald whimpered.

"Trying isn't good enough," Captain Nimbo said with authority.

"Donald, you've got to keep me away from the water," Joe 'Dobe pleaded.

"I'll do my best," the boy answered.

King Crab led the procession through the rocks toward the boat. Stumbling in complete darkness, Joe asked, "How much farther?"

"We're getting there. That's all I know," King Crab answered, stepping in the water that lapped at the path. "Watch your step, Captain. There's water on our right."

Passing the information to the next person

in line, the captain said, "Move to the left, Donald, there's water on the right."

Donald repeated, "Move to the left, Joe. There's water on the right."

Suddenly there was a huge splash. Joe had moved the wrong direction and stepped into a hole full of water. "Help! Quick! Someone help me!" he bellowed.

Captain Nimbo's temper flared as he hollered, "You bumbling dimwit. You went the wrong way."

"Get me out of here. Hurry! My foot's already getting soggy." The sloshing water quickly dissolved his toes, ate away at his heel and weakened his ankle. In order to get out, Joe made a clumsy jump for safety, landing on his fat stomach. But his foot hit the edge of the hole, broke off and fell into the water. The mudman crawled away from the little waves.

Only King Crab could see what was happening, but Donald felt his friend's big head beside him. "Come on Joe, Get off your hands and knees and stand up," the boy pleaded. "King Crab! Captain! Help me!"

"Hoist him on to my shell," King Crab urged. "I'll carry him for a bit."

Feeling their way around, they found Joe's arms and pulled him on to the king's back. Captain Nimbo warned, "Don't fall off, you old horse marine. We don't want any more accidents."

King Crab's seven legs strained under the weight as he carefully drug the mudman farther

on to the dry sand. When they reached the cave wall, Joe steadied himself against it and staggered upright. He balanced on one leg and snickered, "Oh my, I'm a foot short!"

"Here, lean on me, Joe," Donald offered. The mudman used the boy as a crutch and together they moved slowly toward the dock with the captain leading them.

Donald asked with concern, "Does it hurt, Joe?"

"Nope, but now I've really got something to worry about. Can you make me a new foot tonight?"

"I'd like to try, but I'll need more adobe mud," the boy stated.

"There's no adobe in San Francisco. The city was built on sand dunes," Captain Nimbo informed him. "You'll just have to limp for a few days, Joe. We've got to pull the plug before we look for any more mud."

"Let me go back and find his foot. Maybe I can glue it back on," Donald suggested.

But Captain Nimbo disagreed, "Forget it kid. It's a lost cause. You'll never find it in the dark."

Joe 'Dobe complained loudly, "I need a new foot. Now!"

Squeezing his big hand, Donald tried to soothe Joe, "Be patient. Maybe I can think of another way to fix it."

When they reached the ferryboat, Captain Nimbo hurried aboard and turned on the lights. Joe hobbled carefully on to the deck with his arm still around Donald's shoulder. After King

91

Crab untied the ferryboat, he crawled on for the ride across the water. The captain started the engine and they slowly moved through the darkness. The three passengers stood on the auto deck and quietly stared ahead. Breaking the silence, Donald asked, "When are we going to dive?"

"We don't have to go underwater," King Crab answered. "You see, when the tide is in far enough, there's a special entrance that looks like a solid rock wall from the outside. After we pass a certain point inside the cave, the ship will break a laser beam. Then a hidden door will automatically open and we'll pass through. We will suddenly appear on the Bay—almost like magic."

Suggested Activity: *Visit Alcatraz and try to find where you think the entrance to King Crab's grotto might be. Call ahead for reservations and ask for the audio tour. Phone: 415-546-2805 for information. Phone: 415-546-2700 for tickets and reservations.*

Chapter 7

Fisherman's Wharf and Ghirardelli Square

The crew was blinded by the late afternoon sun as the ferryboat emerged from the dark grotto through the hidden passageway. A swift breeze caused white caps to form and the ferryboat bounced on the little waves. When their eyes adjusted to the daylight, Donald was amazed at the activity on the Bay. There were other ferryboats, lots of sailboats, a big tanker and many wind surfers.

Captain Nimbo turned the ship toward San Francisco and in no time they were slowing down for the dock at Fisherman's Wharf. The captain pulled the cord and gave two deep blasts on the horn to announce their arrival, *boooomp, boooomp.* King Crab tied the old ferry to the dock near the red and white boats before he scurried away to find the parts for his power supply. "Enjoy your crab dinner. I'll be back early tomorrow morning," he said, waving good-bye.

Joe limped without help across the auto deck. He picked up the jumbo crab leg and threw it over his broad shoulder. "Let's get going. It will take a while for this to cook and I'm starving!" The three mates left the boat and joined the hustle and bustle of the City.

The wharf area was crowded with visitors from all parts of the world. It was also alive with all kinds of sights, sounds and smells. There were sidewalk vendors selling everything from handmade crafts to unique jewelry and art work. Clowns made balloon animals for the children, white-faced mimes in crazy outfits performed, jugglers threw balls high into the air and a one-man-band entertained them all. The aroma of San Francisco sourdough French bread was mixed with the scent of delicious seafood being prepared at the open air cafes and famous restaurants.

Joe 'Dobe was an attraction himself. Tourists watched as the massive mudman led his friends down the busy sidewalk. He walked unevenly with the giant crab leg balanced on his shoulder. They stared and snapped pictures as he limped through the crowd. When he finally located an empty crab cooker, he shouted in his deep voice, "Excuse me folks, I'm coming through!"

A stout man with pure white hair wiped his hands on his dirty apron as Joe approached. "Well, if it isn't Joe 'Dobe," he shouted over the noise of the traffic and the tourists. "Where in the world have you been keeping yourself? I haven't seen you for years!"

"I fell overboard at the North Pole and was just rebuilt in Santa Cruz," the mudman explained.

"Clear the cookers, men. Joe 'Dobe is back and he's got a leg from King Crab!"

"Thanks," Joe said gratefully. "I was afraid I wasn't going to find a place to cook tonight. Yup, it's sure busy down here."

"It's like this every night," the man said. He cut the crab leg into thirds and dropped one section in each of three crab cookers. While they waited for it to cook, he inquired, "How is King Crab, anyhow?"

"Kingly, as usual," Joe replied. "It was good to see him again. and I'm sure looking forward to a taste of this leg of his."

Leaving Joe on the crowded walkway, Captain Nimbo and Donald climbed the steps to Alioto's, a famous seafood restaurant overlooking the fishing boats. The captain went right to the kitchen door as if he owned the place. "Look alive in there. Tell your cook that Captain Nimbo is here and needs a salad big enough for Joe 'Dobe, plus a little more for the two of us." He pointed at the boy and himself. "He'll know what to do."

They waited until an elderly cook dressed in a white apron and a chef's hat delivered an enormous green salad. "I used the largest bowl I have," the cook said. "The salad is on the house. If Joe 'Dobe wants more, tell him to come get it himself. I'd like to see him again."

"Thanks," Captain Nimbo said.

"Thank you," the boy repeated. They waved good-bye and hurried across the street to the

Boudin Bakery, where they bought nine round loaves of warm French bread. With bread to eat, Donald knew he wouldn't go hungry because he was certain he was not going to eat any of King Crab's leg.

Since they were carrying the huge bowl of salad and the sacks of bread, Captain Nimbo and Donald had trouble making their way through the large group of people that had gathered around Joe. The mudman was shaking hands with the children and repeating in his booming voice, "Everyone come tomorrow. See a once-in-a-life time event. Captain Nimbo and I will be pulling the plug in San Francisco Bay. You'll get to see the Flying Ferry Boat. It will happen about noon, so bring a picnic lunch and sit by the water. You are all invited."

Donald set down his bags of bread and wiggled his way to Joe's side. He grabbed the big mud hand and said, "Come on. Get the cooked crab and let's go back to the ferryboat." However, Joe was enjoying being the center of attention, so he was not ready to leave. Donald gave his hand another tug and said loudly, "Joe, it's time to eat!"

The word *eat* finally caught the mudman's ear. "Is that crab about ready?" he asked.

Nodding, the man at the cooker removed the pieces of leg from the big pots and rinsed them. Wiping his hands on his apron, he carefully cracked one piece at a time with his rubber mallet and expertly wrapped the crab in white paper. He handed all the packages to Joe 'Dobe.

Joe patted the man on the shoulder in friendship. "Thanks, buddy!"

The man replied, "Enjoy your dinner and come back when you can stay longer."

Juggling the three large packages, Joe limped clumsily toward the boat. "It's sure good to be back on Fisherman's Wharf," he commented happily.

Following close behind with the sacks full of bread, Donald asked, "How come these old guys down here know you, Joe?"

"Oh, the captain and I used to tie up to this pier and eat here all the time. These guys were my buddies. Yup, they all remember me because I could eat more crab than anyone else!"

Back on the ferryboat, Joe heaped the cooked crab on a platter and began melting butter to make his favorite lemon-butter sauce. Donald poured dressing on the salad and tossed it while Captain Nimbo sliced the bread.

They carried the meal to the table and sat down together. Captain Nimbo handed them each a fork and an empty plate. "Pull your ears back and eat to the full, mates," he said enthusiastically.

Donald's stomach churned and he made a terrible face as he looked at the pounds of crab in the center of the table. "What's the matter, kid? You look like your stomach is full of flying fish," Captain Nimbo laughed.

"I don't eat crab."

"Here," Joe encouraged, placing a small piece of crab leg on Donald's plate. The boy slowly stuck his fork inside the shell and pulled out a piece of meat. "Now dip it in this sauce," the mudman directed. Donald closed his eyes and reluctantly put the bite in his mouth. The delicate texture and flavor surprised him. He actually liked it.

Joe 'Dobe ate a lot of crab, bread and salad, stuffing it in so fast that he could barely catch his breath. When all the food was gone, he pushed his chair back, propped his footless leg on a stool and announced loudly, "Now I need something sweet. Yup, something like a hot fudge sundae."

"Ghirardelli's Chocolate Manufactory is the best place in San Francisco for a hot fudge sundae," Captain Nimbo said with a smile. "As far as I'm concerned, they've got the best chocolate anywhere on the seven seas."

"Where is this place?" Joe asked.

"At the old chocolate factory—at least a mile from here. Are you up for a walk, mate?"

"Nope. Not with only one foot."

"Could we take one of those funny cars I saw?" Donald asked. "The ones with a seat in back and someone pedaling in front."

"Good idea, kid," Captain Nimbo agreed.

Joe 'Dobe's mouth began watering as he thought about the taste of hot fudge. "Well, what are we waiting for? Let's go." The mudman limped down the gangplank and led the way to a group of pedal-cabs. He awkwardly hopped in the first one, completely filling the seat and straining the axle.

Donald and Captain Nimbo jumped in the one behind. "Haul 'round to Ghirardelli Square," the captain ordered. The two bicyclists pedaled through the crowded streets, weaving among the cars and pedestrians.

Joe was so heavy that his cab fell behind. "Hey, wait for me," he called.

Captain Nimbo yelled back, "Easy there, mate. There's lots of ice cream and hot fudge where we're going."

The bicyclist hauling Joe was sweating and breathing hard when he arrived at the foot of the stairs at Ghirardelli Square. "He's probably the heaviest sailor you'll ever haul. You've earned every penny of this," Captain Nimbo commented when he paid the driver.

Looking at the climb ahead, Joe shouted to the night sky, "I need a new foot." He held on to the metal banister and slowly struggled up the long flight of steps, stopping to rest on all the landings.

The line outside the Ghirardelli Chocolate Manufactory reached as far as the mermaid fountain. A waiter brought everyone a menu to read while they waited. When they were close to the order desk, Captain Nimbo asked, "How many sundaes do you want, Joe?"

The mudman peeked through the glass door to see how big they were, then answered, "Only twenty-two. Please have them make the kind with vanilla ice cream, lots of hot fudge, whipped cream, nuts and a cherry on top."

"Twenty-two!!" Donald blurted. "How can

you eat that much?"

"I'm on a seafood diet. When I see food, I eat it!" Joe joked.

Much to the waiter's surprise, Captain Nimbo ordered twenty-four hot fudge sundaes and only three spoons. Donald looked around while they waited for their order to be ready. He was curious about the ovens that roasted the chocolate beans and the vats which were automatically mixing the melted chocolate. He stopped by the serving counter to watch the sundae-makers in their tall chef's hats pour the thick hot fudge on sundae after sundae. He wandered through the adjoining gift shop and noticed all the candy bars and cable cars made of molded chocolate.

When their number was called, Captain Nimbo went to the fountain to pick up their order. It took several trips to bring the trays full of sundaes to their table. Joe immediately started eating. "You're right. These are the best sundaes in the world! Keep them coming, Captain."

While Donald was eating, he couldn't stop thinking about all the kinds of chocolate he had seen. Suddenly he slapped the table and announced, "I've got an idea, Joe. Maybe I can fix your foot tonight."

Joe gulped another big spoonful of ice cream and then asked, "Tonight? How?"

"I might be able to make you a chocolate foot."

"Really?"

"Yeah, it could work."

"Wait a minute. Let me finish eating first," Joe said firmly. He ate steadily, setting the empty sundae glasses down on the table, as he finished one after another. He said nothing more until he had eaten them all. "OK, Dr. Donald. I'm ready!"

Donald took Joe's big hand and led him over to the marble serving counter. "I'd like to talk to the head chocolate-maker, please," he requested.

One of the cooks swung the kitchen door opened and called, "Hey, Chief, someone here would like to talk with you."

Soon a man with a wrinkled face rushed through the door. He was wearing a clean white apron with the word *Chief* embroidered across the front.

"Sir," Donald began, "my friend here needs a new foot. I'm wondering if we could make him a chocolate one."

The cook listened carefully as Donald explained his idea. "Well," said the experienced candy-maker, rubbing his brow and obviously thinking things through, "we do make chocolate coins and cable cars, so I don't think a foot would be impossible."

Listening to the conversation, Captain Nimbo said, "Let's hoist away then and give her a try." Joe nodded his head in agreement.

The elderly cook took charge and adjusted the recipe to make a larger quantity. He measured the ingredients into a big copper kettle. As the chocolate melted and began to bubble, the candy-maker checked the temperature and kept a watchful eye on the boiling pot.

When it was time, he added cupful after cupful of finely ground oatmeal to strengthen the mixture. His white cook's hat bounced and dark chocolate splattered on his apron as he worked. "With or without nuts?" he questioned, stirring briskly.

"Without nuts, please," Donald answered.

After it had simmered for a while, he gave a ready signal. It took two cooks to lift the heavy kettle and pour the chocolate on to the long marble counter. Donald pulled on a pair of vinyl gloves to protect him from the hot chocolate and worked rapidly, pushing and patting the special mixture into a foot shape.

When the chocolate foot matched the mud one, Donald told Joe to swing his leg up on the counter. He also asked the chief candy-maker to smear a thick layer of chocolate on the stump of Joe's leg. "Watch your balance now, Joe," the boy cautioned. The cooks helped lift the new foot into place and pressed it gently on to the sticky surface of the stub.

Joe had a silly smile on his face. He kept one hand on Captain Nimbo's shoulder to steady himself, but suddenly he began chuckling. "Fudge Foot. Yup, you can just call me Fudge Foot."

"Keep still, Joe," the boy gently scolded. "Your whole body shakes when you laugh. Do you want to end up with a crooked foot?"

"Well, you're tickling me," Joe said as he

moved again.

Donald smoothed on an outer coating of melted chocolate. Like a doctor putting on a plaster cast, he covered the adobe all the way to the mudman's calf to seal the connection. He warned his friend a second time, "Joe, you can't budge until this chocolate sets up."

Looking at his watch, the head cook gently tested the thickest part of the foot by pressing on the candy with his thumb. "OK, Joe. It's hard enough. You can stand up now."

The mudman slid his leg off the marble slab and cautiously put weight on his new foot. He wiggled his dark brown toes and rocked back and forth. "It feels pretty good to me. Yup, maybe better than the old one," he announced, grinning broadly.

Donald watched intently and then said, "Try taking a few small steps."

"OK, Dr. Donald." Joe walked hesitantly across the restaurant. With every step the mudman gained more confidence in his new foot. "You're a genius, mate!" he exclaimed.

The captain looked at the young landlubber with new respect. "Well, I'll be a fish's fin! That was a great idea, kid," he acknowledged.

The spellbound customers clapped and cheered. Donald let out the biggest whoop of all, proud that his plan had worked.

The crew thanked the chief chocolate-maker and shook hands with the whole line of aproned cooks. "Bye, everyone and thanks!" Joe called as they left. He was happy because his belly was full of chocolate sundaes and he was walking on two feet again.

They left the ice cream parlor, walked under the arched sign with the lights that spelled GHIRARDELLI and hiked down the steep hill in the moonlight. Soon Joe was striding along, taking giant steps in his usual bumbling fashion, forcing Captain Nimbo and Donald to run as they made their way back to the ferryboat.

Once on board, Captain Nimbo went directly to the pilot house to check the computer. While they were waiting for the captain to return, Joe set up a game of dominoes and explained the rules to his young friend. The crew played several rounds before turning in. It was a good way to end an exciting day.

It was late when Joe showed Donald to a small cabin. The mudman pulled back the blankets and fluffed the pillow. "Sleep tight," he said, giving the boy a big hug. Donald lay down on lower bunk bed and quickly slipped into a dreamless sleep, happy to have a friend like Joe.

When Joe poked his head into the captain's cabin to say good night, the seaman was setting his alarm for 5:30 A.M. The drowsy captain told Joe, "Have a good night's sleep, mate. We have to be shipshape for tomorrow."

"Aye, aye, Captain. Are you sure everything's ready?"

"As sure as I can be," Captain Nimbo sleepily answered. "If the *Law of Imbuggerance* doesn't come into effect, we'll be fine."

Joe dimly remembered the old law of the sea

that says, *"Things always happen at the worst time and in the worst place."* However, he was too happy with his new foot to worry about what more could happen. He crawled into his familiar bunk, closed his eyes and soon his heavy snoring was vibrating the whole room.

Suggested Activity: *Go and see the crab cookers at Fisherman's Wharf. Try a bite of crab. While you're there, visit the Boudin Bakery and ride the elevator up to Alioto's restaurant. Then go have a world famous hot fudge sundae at the Ghirardelli Chocolate Manufactory.*

Chapter 8

Pulling the Plug

It was still dark when Captain Nimbo's alarm clock went off. He unkinked his long body and climbed out of his bunk. "Rise and shine, you lazy landlubbers. Today's the day we pull the plug," he called to his sleeping crew. Wearing his captain's hat with his pajamas, he headed to the pilot house. The computer showed that the gate was almost closed, sealing off San Francisco Bay from the ocean. He contacted the Coast Guard to be certain they were ready and also checked with the news media to make sure that the warning was still being broadcast. Finishing these important tasks, he returned to his cabin and got dressed. Afterwards, he found Joe in the galley brewing a pot of coffee and asked, "Well, mate, any questions about your job today?"

"Just like before, I'm in charge of the hook, right?"

"Right—and we'll pull the plug at noon."

"Yup . . . and I hope some sailor who didn't hear the news doesn't get in our way."

"Me, too, Captain Nimbo agreed, "and no

doubt there will be at least one foolish fish who goes down the drain rather than following King Crab's directions to leave the bay." The captain poured himself a mug of strong coffee and talked with Joe while he fixed breakfast. He wanted Joe to have plenty energy, so he dumped two large containers of rolled oats into a huge pan, then added several quarts of water and a measure of salt. He briskly stirred the cereal and, while it cooked, he cut up some fresh fruit and put bread in the toaster.

When Donald appeared in the mess hall, he had a big a smile on his face. "I love sleeping in my clothes. I'm already dressed. Mom's always bugging me about taking a bath and putting on fresh clothes. What's the big deal about being clean anyway?"

The captain replied with a twinkle in his eye, "Well, mate, if you never washed or changed your clothes, you'd really smell. I'd call you a stink pot myself." All three of them laughed.

"I wish I was made of mud," Donald said. "Joe's lucky. He never stinks. He doesn't wear clothes, so he doesn't have to change them. And he never has to take a shower. If he did, he would soon be a huge mud puddle."

"You could clone yourself in mud, Donald. After all, you're quite a sculptor," the captain remarked.

"Mmmm, maybe I will," Donald responded.

Scurrying back and forth from the galley, Captain Nimbo put the hot cereal, fresh fruit, and toast on the table. "Eat hearty, mates!" he commanded.

"Yup, I'm starved again," Joe said, licking his lips.

Offering the pan of cereal to Donald first, the captain said, "Help yourself to some cream of cement. It'll stick to your ribs all day."

The young boy knew a busy time was ahead, so he filled his bowl with hot oatmeal, even though he would have preferred sugary cereal with milk. After serving himself, the captain gave the rest of the huge amount to Joe. Using the largest spoon in the galley, Joe hungrily shoveled the oatmeal into his mouth, emptying the big pan. He also ate several loaves of whole-wheat toast with honey and most of the fruit. At last he patted his round belly, pushed his chair back from the table and said, "Good grub, Captain. Come on, Donald, let's clean up the galley before the king gets here."

Captain Nimbo drank a third cup of coffee while they waited for King Crab. Tapping his foot and puffing impatiently on his pipe, he fumed, "Where *is* that smelly hunk of crab meat? He was supposed to be here an hour ago."

Before long there was loud pounding from below. "Hey! It's time to work. Let's get a move on, Captain!" King Crab called, as he beat his pincers on the side of the boat. "I order you to hurry up!"

"OK, Hold on. I'll be there in a second!" Captain Nimbo grumbled. "That crab! He knows I don't like to be ordered around. He's late and then he wants me to hurry." Angrily, the captain stomped up to the pilot house. He opened the window and snarled at the big crab, "You could have been on time. They do make waterproof watches, you know."

King Crab called back, "I took the time to make sure all the sea life had left the Bay."

"How about the crabs who will be cleaning the shoreline?" the captain questioned. "Are they following your orders?"

"Of course. They'll be sitting on Angel Island, ready and waiting," the king replied. "But the Bay is such a mess, the crabs can't possibly clean it up by themselves."

"I already thought of that," Captain Nimbo responded smugly. "I got the mayor to let all the schools out tomorrow. There will be lots of small landlubbers working all around the Bay to pick up the trash."

"That's great. Now if there's nothing more, I'm off to find the plug for you," the king said.

"Don't bother. I've programmed my computer to do that. Why don't you hop on board and ride out with us?"

"Pardon me? I need to follow the tradition of former crab kings. It is my duty to locate the plug and guide you to it. Therefore, I am going to do that." King Crab waved his big claw toward the middle of the Bridge. "Take your boat out there and wait for me." He *splaaaashed* into the water and quickly disappeared, leaving a trail of rising bubbles.

The captain shrugged his shoulders and

commented, "OK, King, do it yourself, but there is an easier way." He turned from the window and started the ferryboat engine. The motor coughed and choked a few times before settling into its normal rumble. When he steered the ferryboat away from Fisherman's Wharf, they could see the huge golden dam shining brightly in the early morning sunlight. It kept the tide from flowing in or out, so the Bay was unusually calm.

Donald entered the pilot house and climbed on to the empty swivel chair beside the captain. He immediately asked another question. "Where is the plug, anyhow?"

Without a complaint, Captain Nimbo explained that it was located in the very deepest part of the Bay, about 350 feet down, right in the bottom of an underwater canyon. "That canyon goes underneath the Golden Gate Bridge. We'll be above it shortly."

"Oh, boy!" Donald replied, eager for more action to start.

"Where's Joe?" the captain asked.

"He went down to the auto deck to check the hook." As the ferryboat chugged on to the Bay, Donald noticed many people along the waterfront. Some were walking around with cameras or binoculars; others were unfolding chairs or spreading out blankets. Apparently they heard or read the news and had come to watch.

Reaching the middle of the Bay, the captain called over the intercom, "How's everything down below, Joe?"

"The hook is in good shape, but this other stuff needs some lubricating," Joe reported.

"Do you think it will give us any problems?" the captain questioned.

Joe answered from the auto deck, "Hard to say."

"Why do you have your fingers crossed, Captain?" Donald asked.

"Well, I've rigged up this old equipment as best I can. I have a better chance than most at getting the job done, but things do go wrong, you know." The captain stopped the ferryboat above the underwater canyon. While they waited there for King Crab, a flock of sea gulls circled overhead, screeching for scraps of food for their breakfast. Impatient, the captain asked over the intercom, "Joe, do you see the king yet?"

"Nope," Joe answered, looking into the murky water.

"He should have found that plug by now," the captain complained.

"He'll come up sooner or later."

"He had better be quick about it." Captain Nimbo grew more restless and finally lit his pipe, blowing clouds of smoke above his head.

"Hey, Captain, is that King Crab?" Donald asked, pointing out the window.

"Where? I don't see him," the captain grumbled, grabbing his binoculars.

"Way over there." Donald motioned, pointing toward the southern shore by Fort Point.

"That's him all right. I wonder what he's

doing?" The boat chugged across the water to King Crab, who was sitting on a big rock close to the gold gate. "What's the matter?" Captain Nimbo called through the opened window. "You've had more than enough time to find the plug."

The crab king was annoyed by the captain's comment, but he tried to be polite. "Mr. Nimbo, if you please, I'm very upset at the moment."

"Well," grouched the captain in a loud voice, "now what is it?"

The big crab lost his temper. "If you'd open your eyes instead of your mouth, you'd see what the problem is," he sneered. "It was so dirty down there, I could barely see my claws in front of me and some of them got wrapped up in a bunch of junk. I crawled over here to untangle myself."

Disregarding his complaints, the captain asked, "You found the plug, didn't you?"

"No, that's the worse part. I couldn't find it," groaned the crab.

"You couldn't find it! Come on, you're kidding me, aren't you? You said you had to do this yourself, so get with it, King. You're burning daylight and we've got lots to do. Besides, that plug is about the size of a city block. With all of your legs, I'm surprised you didn't trip over it."

King Crab picked off another tangle of wire mixed with seaweed before defending himself. "I know I must have been on top of it, but it's probably covered with barnacles or just buried under the mess down there."

The captain barked, "Then look for the loop, you ninny. It's sticking straight up."

"What does it look like?" Donald inquired.

Captain Nimbo took a pencil from his desk drawer. He quickly drew a picture that looked like a short nail with a wedding ring sitting on it. The loop was centered in something that reminded Donald of an old-fashioned bathtub plug. The captain leaned out of the window and yelled to the crab, "Give up, Your Majesty. My Mebus 21 will easily find the plug."

The king shook his big claw at the captain and sniffed, "I know I can do better than a machine that can't even think by itself." The big crab cleaned off the last bit of rubbish from his seventh leg. Still determined to find the plug, he ignored the captain, crawled down the rocks and disappeared into the water.

Not liking the tension, Donald bit his fingernails and asked the captain, "What if King Crab gets caught in something again?"

Captain Nimbo shrugged his shoulders and said loudly, "That's his problem. Besides, that old dripper can take care of himself."

Joe called from the lower deck, "Yup, I'm sure he'll do just fine."

Captain Nimbo slammed the window and sprung into action. He turned to his computer and quickly brought up his new program. "That old crab doesn't like being replaced by a machine, but I'm going to show him what my Mebus 21 can do. Watch this, Donald, I'm setting the coordinates. My Mebus does the soundings electronically. There, see that curved image coming into focus? That's the loop on the plug. That's what we're looking for."

Donald was impressed. "You sure did that fast."

"Yes, I know. King Crab will hate to admit that a machine works better than he does. We found the plug, so let's go pull it."

Captain Nimbo called over the intercom to Joe, "We're shoving off, mate." The captain shifted the boat into gear and guided it toward the deeper water, following the course laid out by the Mebus 21. When they reached a spot near the loop, he shut down the engines so he could convert the ferryboat into a submarine. He activated the clear plastic bubble to encase the boat, slowly filled the ballast tanks and performed the pressure tests. When he was certain there were no leaks, he sounded the warning horn, *hoooonk, hoooonk, hoooonk* and ordered Donald to push the DIVE button. They easily sank beneath the water. Soon the captain commanded, "Joe, ready the hook."

"Aye, aye, captain," Joe's loud voice boomed from below.

The deeper they went, the darker it got, so Captain Nimbo turned on the outer lights. The propeller churned *rrrr, rrrr, rrrr, rrrr*, thrusting them steadily down into the underwater canyon. The computer screen showed the area in front of them and guided their descent. It also let them know the depth of the submarine and the distance to the plug. "Hey, mates, the metal

115

ring should be directly in front of us." Captain Nimbo slowed the engine. "Can you see it yet?"

All Donald could see was murky dark-green water as he peered through the plastic bubble. He looked up and down, then right and left. In time he yelled excitedly, "There it is! Wow! Look at that!"

"Good work, Donald." The captain quickly brought the submarine to a stop. "Now go point it out to Joe."

Donald ran down the series of stairs shouting, "Joe, Joe, I've found the loop."

During this time the mudman had been on the auto deck oiling the equipment that had sat idle for so long. Joe was scratching his head and fumbling with the hook mechanism, struggling to move the control lever. He muttered, "Uh, come on you stupid dooflicker."

"Joe, the loop's right in front of us!" Donald exclaimed.

"So what? If the hook won't work, we're not pulling any plug," the mudman mumbled, without even looking up.

Soon the captain's voice called over the intercom, "Come on, Joe. I've got the boat level. Hook her up."

"I would, if I could," Joe called back. "We've got a problem down here, Captain. The lever is stuck."

"Oops. I forgot to tell you that I put in a locking pin."

"Huh? A what?"

"A locking pin. It's located under the hook."

The captain went on to explain, "You see, the hook was wearing a hole in the bow because it kept swinging around and banging the same spot over and over. That little pin holds it in place."

Joe and Donald examined the hook and eventually found a metal pin attached to a short cable. The mudman laughed, "My fat fingers will never fit in that little space. See if you can get it out, Donald." The boy reached down, tugged on the cable with all his might and pulled out the pin.

Joe yanked the lever and reported, "It works, by golly. Thanks, Donald."

"You're very welcome, Joe," the boy answered, pleased that he had been able to help again.

In a booming voice the mudman called over the intercom, "OK, Captain. Now we're ready for hookup."

Donald pointed out the location of the metal ring in the cloudy water. With the control arm, Joe 'Dobe began gently maneuvering the giant hook forward. The submarine drifted slightly in the water, making it hard to hook the ring. "Move to the right about three feet," Donald directed. "Now move down, now go forward." The boy watched every attempt, holding his breath as Joe got close and being disappointed when he missed. Finally he yelled, "You've got it, Joe. You've got it!"

"Yup, I do." Joe 'Dobe wiped the sweat from his forehead. "We've hooked her, Captain. Pull the plug!" he shouted.

Immediately Captain Nimbo put the boat into reverse and applied power. The boat pulled on the plug, but nothing happened. The captain gave the boat more power and tugged again. Still the gigantic plug did not move.

"I thought it would just pop out when the ferryboat pulled on it," Donald commented.

"It has before," Joe responded. "I don't know what's wrong. Let's go upstairs and join the captain." They gripped the banister and balanced against the walls as the boat lurched forward and back.

"This dumb plug, it's stuck like tar on a sailor's bare foot!" Captain Nimbo bellowed as they entered the pilot house.

"How come?" Donald asked.

"How should I know? I'm hoping it'll break loose if I keep up the pressure," Captain Nimbo said. He continued to pull on the plug.

Donald held on tightly to the back of the chair as the boat jerked with each pull. Staring out the window, he remembered something and quickly suggested, "When the plug in our bathtub was stuck, my dad yanked it real hard, straight up."

The captain, thinking intently, repeated to himself, "Mmmm. Real hard, straight up." He spit on his hands, then rubbed them together and said, "OK, mates. Strap yourselves into your seats. I'm going to try your dad's way, Donald, but I have to put the sub on her nose."

Moving directly above the ring, the captain

reset the controls. The boat immediately lurched forward, tipping downward. Donald and Joe hung face down in their seat belts. Jamming the engine into full-reverse, the captain gave the plug a series of violent jerks. "Wow, this feels like a ride at Disneyland, only it's for real!" Donald gasped.

"It feels like an upside-down earthquake to me," Joe groaned.

Captain Nimbo felt the plug loosen, so he let up on the throttle. Unfortunately the chain sagged and the plug fell back into place. On the second try, he maintained full power, kept constant pressure on the chain and pulled straight up.

POP!! . . . At last the plug came out, followed by a strange sucking sound, *fluuuu.* A gigantic *whoooosh* of water swirled down the drain. The submarine shot upward, dragging the plug through the water.

Donald gave a cheer. "Hooray! Hooray! We pulled the plug!!"

Joe chuckled at the boy's excitement. "Yup, we got it out at last!"

The captain warned, "Be serious, men. It's not time to celebrate yet. We're in a dangerous place. We've got to get ourselves and the plug out of here before we get washed down the hole. Now hang on!"

Still in reverse, he rapidly powered the sub away from the underwater whirlpool. They dumped the water from the ballast tanks and shot stern first on to the water's surface. The

submarine briefly floated high above the drain while Captain Nimbo hurried to convert her into a regular ferryboat.

He nervously stroked his beard as he waited for the panels to unlock and disappear. Then he quickly pressed the FLY button, which activated the telescoping wings, transforming the ferryboat into an airplane. As soon as he could, he hauled the plug high above the water and flew toward shore.

"Wow, that was neat! We just changed from a sub, to a boat, to an airplane. Now can we celebrate, Captain?" Donald asked.

"Sure," Captain Nimbo replied, "but do it quickly. We don't have far to go."

Jumping happily around the pilot house, Donald hugged Joe. Then without thinking, he turned and hugged the captain, too. Joe 'Dobe grinned from ear to ear and said, "We did it! Once again we pulled the plug. King Crab will certainly be flabbergasted!"

The mention of the crab's name reminded Donald that the king was still underwater. "What about King Crab? Won't he go down the drain!"

Captain Nimbo slumped in his chair. "Oh, blast! Dagnab it! I forgot all about him. I was too busy trying to prove what my computer could do. I sure hope he got out of the way." He knew the whirlpool would grow more and more powerful as the water level dropped.

Joe frowned, bit his lower lip and sadly said, "Nope, we can't do anything to help him now."

The large white ferryboat flew slowly toward San Francisco with the gigantic concrete plug swinging beneath it. As the water emptied out, more of the real golden gate appeared, gleaming in the sunlight. Far below them, gallons of sea water rushed down the drain, swirling like a liquid tornado.

Suggested Activity: *Park at Crissy Field in the Presidio and walk along the sandy shoreline toward the Golden Gate Bridge. Visit Fort Point. Phone: 415-556-1693. If you are really ambitious, follow the steep path up the hillside and walk across the Bridge. The deepest part of the Bay is just to the north of the middle of the Bridge.*

Chapter 9

A Dangerous Rescue

The midday sun shone through the window on the mismatched crew—a salty old sea captain, a gentle giant of a mudman and a young wide-eyed boy. Donald pressed his nose against the window to watch the water as it began to move in a big circle. Suddenly something caught his attention. "Joe, what's that? See that yellow thing out there?"

Joe squinted in the direction Donald was pointing. "Where?"

"Over there. It looks like a long fish, but it's staying on top of the water."

Peering through binoculars, Joe yelled, "Oh, no! It's a kayak. Have a look, Captain." He handed the high powered glasses to his friend.

"Holy octopus!" Captain Nimbo yowled when he spotted the dot of yellow. "This time we've got a stupid kayaker instead of a stupid fish. There's always someone who doesn't listen."

"Yup, and we're the only ones who can save them." Joe groaned.

As they talked, the kayak drifted steadily toward the drain site, even though the paddler was trying to go the opposite direction. But before they could attempt a rescue, Captain Nimbo had to set down the heavy plug, so he quickly flew to Crissy Field. Everyone—runners, bicyclists, kite fliers, even dogs—scurried to get out of the way as the big boat hovered over the asphalt at the old air base. The captain slowly lowered the huge plug on to the pavement, knocking over a few fences in the process. Joe returned to the auto deck to unhook the enormous piece of concrete. Donald followed, eager to help.

As soon as the plug was disconnected, Captain Nimbo called over the loud speaker. "Now we've got to get that kayaker out of the water." He turned the Flying Ferry Boat around and flew over the Bay at a low altitude.

They could see that the kayak was moving rapidly toward the open drain, looking like an autumn leaf floating down a rushing stream. Circling above, the captain opened his window and shouted, "You've got to get out of here."

The kayaker's paddle blades were flashing in the sunlight. "I'm trying to get to shore. What in the world is going on?" a woman yelled at the top of her lungs. "I've never seen such crazy currents in the Bay."

Joe 'Dobe leaned over the side and shouted, "We pulled the plug. Didn't you hear the news?"

"No. I've just spent a week paddling down the Sacramento River," the silver-haired woman shouted back.

The captain hollered from above, "You should have stayed there. At least you'd be safe."

"Look here, I've been in raging waters before. I even took this little kayak through the Grand Canyon," she responded, still paddling with all her strength.

"I don't care where you've been, lady. You've got to get out of here, right now," the captain ordered. "You'll be sucked down the drain!"

"Then land beside me and I'll crawl aboard."

Captain Nimbo hovered above the yellow kayak and hooted, "No way! Are you nuts? We'd go down the drain with you!"

"Well, then throw me a life line," she yelled.

Captain Nimbo tried to keep the Flying Ferry Boat close to the kayak. "Quick, Joe. Throw her a rope. Use the one with the harness."

"Aye, aye, Captain." Joe swung the rope several times and then flung it toward the kayak. "Here it comes, lady."

Stretching to reach the harness, the woman leaned too far and her little boat tipped over. She automatically grabbed the side of her boat and held on to the paddle. As she bobbed in her yellow life jacket, the current moved her closer to the dangerous whirlpool.

Fearfully, Donald cried out, "Oh no! She's going to die!"

Working quickly, Joe pulled the rope back on the deck and called over the intercom, "I missed her and she's almost to the whirlpool. Stay with her, Captain. I've got to get the harness to her!"

Again Joe swung the long rope in her direction. On the second throw it landed directly in front of the kayak. The lady dropped everything and swam strongly to the harness, quickly putting her arms through it.

"She's got it!" Donald yelled. He hurried to help hoist the woman on deck. As they were hauling her up, her hat came off and fell into the current next to the kayak. Her possessions were instantly sucked into the shallow hole that had developed in the center of the swirling waters. Donald knew she would have gone down with them if Joe's aim had not been on target.

The mudman called, "Head for shore, Captain! We've got her on board!"

The Flying Ferry Boat flew at a low altitude back to Crissy Field. Captain Nimbo lowered the landing gear and expertly landed the flying boat on the abandoned runway. After shutting down the computer and the overheated engines, he heaved a big sigh of relief and went to join his mates in the living area. "That was a close call. How's the kayaker, Joe?"

"Wet and cold, and she's got scrapes and a bruise or ten from our pulling her on board. Right now she's in the washroom."

In a few minutes the soaked woman entered the room with her hair wrapped in a towel. She had removed her yellow life vest and walking shoes, but still wore her moist socks and a damp vest over her drip-dry clothing. "Boy, I was in over my head this time, gentlemen. Thank you so much for pulling me out!"

"Well, we couldn't let you go down the drain,

could we?" Joe chuckled. "Who are you anyway?"

With a big smile, she said, "People call me
Grani Ann. I manufacture kayaks and take
people on river trips. I was checking out the
Sacramento River for a trip that's coming up."
Joe 'Dobe, Donald and Captain Nimbo intro-
duced themselves and they all shook hands.
Then she questioned, "What was going on out
there today?"

"We pulled the plug to drain San Francisco
Bay," Captain Nimbo responded.

"I've lived here all my life, but I've never
heard anything about a plug in the Bay."

"Well, bet your sand dollars, it's there. And
we just pulled it. You could have gone down the
drain with your kayak," the captain scolded.

Realizing what might have happened, Grani
Ann wrapped her arms around herself and
shivered. "Does this mean my kayak—and my
favorite blue hat—are gone forever?"

"I'm afraid so," Joe confirmed. "You were
lucky to get out alive."

Donald piped up, "Hey, you look cold, Grani
Ann."

"There's a big wood cooking stove in the
galley. Would you like me to start a fire so you
can warm up?" Joe offered.

She gratefully responded, "Yes, that would
be wonderful. A hot fire would dry these clothes
in no time."

"Speaking of the galley," Joe said, rubbing
his big belly, "Isn't it about time for lunch,

Captain?"

"Is food all you ever think about?" the captain teased.

He gave them his famous Joe 'Dobe grin and answered, "Yup!"

Smiling at all three of them, the silver-haired woman asked mysteriously, "Have any of you ever eaten raspbannies?"

"I'll eat anything," Joe replied, licking his lips.

"Oh, no!" Donald said, his eyes rolling back. "I like to eat regular food, like peanut butter and jelly sandwiches."

"Come on, Donald. I think you'll like my raspbannies. I'll need bread, jam, eggs, milk, cream cheese, Captain," Grani Ann stated.

"All that stuff's in the pantry."

"Joe, you get a hot fire going under that griddle," she cheerfully ordered. "I'll dry myself out and cook our lunch at the same time."

"Just be sure to make a platter full of raspbannies for my big stomach," Joe requested.

Soon the galley stove radiated with heat. In a short time Grani Ann was fairly dry and wonderful smells leaked into the dining room. Joe's stomach was growling long before the kayaker announced, "Lunch is served! Get a warm plate and come help yourself."

Joe stacked thirty-three pieces of the double-thick French toast filled with cream cheese and raspberry jam on his large plate. He poured himself a steaming cup of coffee and sat down.

Grani Ann took two raspbannies and seated

herself with the rest of them at the big table. After taking a few bites, she commented, "You certainly *do* eat a lot, Joe. I thought I had cooked too much until I saw you dish up your plate."

"Well, when Joe's around the food disappears like fish into a whale's belly," Captain Nimbo remarked.

Joe patted his round stomach happily, "Yup. These are mighty good."

Donald added, "I guess I like raspbannies, after all. They're a lot like a hot peanut butter and jelly sandwich without the peanut butter."

Knowing that there was little to do until the Bay was drained, they relaxed and sat around the table telling stories. Grani Ann related some of her adventures in the Grand Canyon and explained how she manufactured the Kiwi Kayaks. Donald described building Joe. The captain gave some history of the ferryboat and told about the first time they pulled the plug. Joe simply ate and ate, not saying a word, then fell asleep.

Leaving the mudman to rest, the other three washed the dishes. Soon, Grani Ann left for Santa Rosa to pick up another bright yellow kayak because she could hardly stand to be out of the water for more than a day or two. She promised to be back the next afternoon for the cleanup party and thanked them again for rescuing her.

When Joe awoke, he and Donald headed out along the sandy shoreline toward Fort Point.

They took a steep, winding trail that led them uphill to the parking lot by the Golden Gate Bridge. Joining the tourists, they walked up the concrete ramp past the round souvenir shop and followed the sidewalk to the center of the Bridge.

The two friends watched the whirlpool swirl violently above the massive hole. They hoped to see King Crab, but were disappointed that he was nowhere in sight. When they returned to the ferryboat in the early evening, Captain Nimbo was pacing back and forth, puffing on his pipe. He only said, "I'm worried about the king."

Joe made a pot of soup for supper, but the captain didn't eat much. He looked concerned and couldn't sit still. Later, Donald asked in a low voice, "Is Captain Nimbo all right, Joe?"

"Don't fret about him," Joe told the boy. "He acts like this when something is bothering him."

After a quiet evening and some more games of dominoes, it was time to turn in. Walking toward their cabins, Joe squeezed Donald's hand and said, "Tomorrow's a new day. Yup, King Crab will probably show up for breakfast."

Perking up a bit, Captain Nimbo responded, "Let's hope so."

All three of them were thinking about the missing crab as they drifted off to sleep.

Suggested Activity: *Prepare some raspbannies for breakfast. The recipe is on page 132.*

How to Make Raspbannies

To make 8 Raspbannies you will need:

16	slices of bread
1	8 ounce package of softened cream cheese
1	16 ounce jar of raspberry jam—or whatever kind of jam you like
4	eggs
1	cup of milk
2	Tablespoons of sugar
1/4	teaspoon of salt
4	Tablespoons of margarine, butter or oil

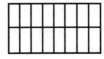

Optional toppings: powdered sugar, butter, syrup

Unwrap the cheese and cut it into 16 equal pieces (see picture above). Lay the bread on the counter and put one pat of cheese on each piece of bread. Carefully spread the cheese, completely covering each piece of bread. Spoon a *heaping* tablespoon of jam in the center of 8 of the breads. Put the remaining cheese-covered bread on top of the bread and jam, cheese sides together. Press the edges all the way around to seal them so the jam doesn't leak out. Gently flatten the middle of each jam sandwich with your hand.

Put the eggs, milk, sugar and salt in a bowl and beat them with a fork until everything is well mixed.

Melt 2 tablespoons of margarine, butter or oil in a large skillet over a medium heat. Dip four jam sandwiches into the egg mixture, completely coating them. Place them in the skillet, put a lid on and cook until golden brown, 2-3 minutes on each side. Do the same with the rest.

Serve with butter and sprinkle with powdered sugar. Some people may also want syrup on top.

Chapter 10

Flying to the North Pole

Early the next morning, before the other two crew members were even thinking about getting out of bed, Captain Nimbo brewed himself a pot of steaming coffee. Nibbling on a handful of sea biscuits and sipping from his mug, he strolled to the Bay's edge, hoping to spot King Crab. As the sun rose, he searched the muddy floor of the Bay with his binoculars, but never saw the king. He did see trash of every kind lying in the soft brown mud. Rubber tires, rusted tin cans, glass bottles, plastic containers, old shoes, discarded toys—all were covered with green, mossy gunk. A small army of tiny crabs was at work, happily munching away the green scum.

Knowing that the Bay would soon be clean, Captain Nimbo smiled one of his rare smiles, then briskly walked back to the ferryboat, shouting as he came into the living area, "Rise and shine, you lazy landlubbers. Get your bones out of those bunks. The crabs are already on the job and time's a'wastin'!"

Jumping out of bed, Donald quickly put on

his shoes, grabbed some food from the galley and hurried outside. Joe followed him and together they gawked at the Bay. It looked like a huge muddy field, with water from the bigger rivers still streaming toward the drain. The boy noticed the crabs chewing on the algae and he almost threw up. "Gross! They're eating that yucky stuff!"

"Who else would clean it up?" Joe 'Dobe questioned. "It's a good thing the crabs like it."

"Look at that junk out there! How come people throw stuff in the Bay?" Donald asked. "When my friends and I grow up we won't do that. I'll tell them about King Crab and the sea life that live in this water."

"Good idea. Yup, you do that, mate."

They walked along the shoreline, hoping to spot the big crab. After a while the school buses began to arrive. Donald told Joe, "I want to work with the kids today. I'll meet you at the boat when we're done, OK?"

"Yup, that's fine with me," Joe agreed.

Eyeing the giant mudman, one of the students asked, "Are we going to look like you pretty soon?"

Joe's fat belly shook with laughter. "Yup, by the end of the day you could look just like me—not as big, but just as muddy!" He walked back to the boat with a big grin on his face.

The children were eager to get started and they followed their teacher's instructions. Everyone got a large orange trash bag and put on a pair of rubber gloves for protection. They

spread out along the shoreline and quickly went to work, dropping slimy junk into the sturdy plastic sacks. Donald got a pair of gloves and joined a group of children about his age. His feet sunk in the soft ooze and he was splattered with sandy mud in no time.

Working side by side, the children chattered.

"I usually hate to pick up trash, but this is fun."

"Yeah! It's better than school, isn't it?"

"I love mud."

"Me, too. This is just great."

"Look at those little crabs."

"My dad said to be careful and watch out for the crabs, but I bet the crabs' dads told them to be careful and watch out for us kids!"

"I wonder if we'll be on the news."

"Isn't it weird to have all the water gone?"

As far as the eye could see, hundreds of students worked in the sandy mud, delighted to be out of school for the day. Piles of orange bags filled with trash soon stretched along the shore.

It was mid-morning when Joe 'Dobe came running toward Donald's group. Out of breath, he shouted, "Hey, Donald, come with me, right now. GASP . . . GASP . . . We've got to go somewhere and GASP . . . GASP . . . the captain's in a big hurry."

Looking confused, Donald slogged as quickly as he could out of the muck, across the sand and through the grass to reach the asphalt pavement. "What's happening?"

Still breathing heavily, Joe answered, "The captain . . . GASP . . . has a surprise."

Enjoying being with the kids, Donald asked, "Can't we go later?"

"Nope." Joe turned and hustled toward the ferryboat. "The captain is ready to go now and he won't wait."

Donald made a quick decision and ran to catch up with Joe. As they got closer to the ferryboat, they heard the captain shout, "Clear the runway." The flying boat began moving slowly away from them.

"Faster, Joe, faster," Donald shouted loudly. "He's leaving without us!"

"Wait, we're coming!" they called, waving their arms. Joe lumbered after the moving boat. Stretching to reach the ladder attached to the side of the hull, he grabbed on to a rung above his head. He quickly grasped Donald's sand-caked arm and strongly lifted the boy on to the ladder, sheltering him as the Flying Ferry Boat left the ground. The wind whistled past their ears as they cautiously climbed to the auto deck of the flying boat.

Joe panted, "Boy, ...GASP...I never could have done that without my fudge foot." The mudman could not understand the captain's impatience. After they climbed the stairs to the pilot house Joe grumbled, "Captain, why didn't you wait? You need our help, you know."

A tower of smoke floated from the captain's pipe as he griped, "Jingo-jango, mates! When it's time, it's time. I can't be sitting around. What took you so long?"

Confused by the change in plans, Donald

answered, "I thought we were going to clean up the Bay today."

The captain grunted, "We've done our part. We pulled the plug and found enough hands to pick up the trash. Besides, it was great to see how fast you two can run."

Captain Nimbo guided the Flying Ferry Boat into the air above the Golden Gate Bridge and headed north. From the window they could see several large cargo ships, a passenger ship and many smaller boats waiting to come into the harbor. The daytime traffic on the Bridge crept more slowly than usual as the drivers tried to catch a glimpse of the waterless Bay. "You see, Donald," the captain explained, "I just got word that an aurora will take place today. That's why we had to leave so quickly."

"Roar-a? What's that?" Donald asked.

"Aurora. The word's *aurora*. I'll tell you about it on the way." Glancing at the boy, the captain remarked, "Go take a peek in the mirror. You look like Joe 'Dobe."

Donald looked down at his shoes and pants, then laughed, "I've never been quite this dirty before."

"Hey, mate, don't get the towels muddy," Captain Nimbo pestered, winking slyly at Joe 'Dobe.

Donald's jaw tightened as he remembered how his mother complained about the mud. But then grinned at the captain, shrugged his shoulders and left the pilot house. When he looked at himself in the bathroom mirror, he saw that he was caked with a mixture of slime, mud and sand. The boy removed his gloves, stuck his head under the faucet and began to wash. He wiped his clothes off as best he could, tucked in his shirt, peeled the muck off his shoes, then washed his hands again. The bathroom was a disaster, but Donald was much cleaner when he rejoined his mates in the pilot house.

The captain announced, "OK, men, take your seats and fasten your seat belts. It's time to head for the North Pole." Excited, Donald buckled up. "Hang on to your hats, mates. I'm shifting into hyper-drive in exactly five seconds. We'll pull a few Gs at first, then we'll cruise along at rocket speed."

The ship shot straight ahead. Flattened against the back of his seat, Donald tried to catch his breath. The blood drained from his face and he felt lightheaded. Noticing his white complexion, Joe said, "Breathe, Donald. Breathe. You'll be OK in a minute." When the color had returned to the boy's face, the mud-man explained their hasty trip. "The captain wants to capture some lights and decorate the City before the cleanup party tonight. Yup, these lights make great special effects."

Donald was excited. "What lights? What city? What decorations?"

"Well, you see, we're going to bring some of the aurora—also called the northern lights— back to decorate San Francisco. There's going to be a big *We Cleaned Up the Bay* party for all the people who helped today. These lights will look beautiful reflected in the clean water, and they make the City glow like a giant Christmas tree on a foggy night."

"You're kidding!?"

"I knew you'd say that. Yup, that's the truth."

Donald was curious, "How do you catch these lights?"

Joe grinned, "We just suck them up with the big vacuum hidden under the auto deck. It's another machine the captain dreamed up."

After the Flying Ferry Boat reached its top speed, the old seaman unhooked his seat belt and said, "Go get the vacuum hoses ready, Joe!"

Getting up from his chair, the first mate called, "Come on, Donald. I can use your help."

Captain Nimbo dismissed them with a wave of his hand, but quickly jumped out of his chair and ran after them ordering, "Hey, Joe! Use those life lines I rigged up. I don't want any men overboard this time."

"We will, Captain."

"Someone fell overboard?" Donald asked on their way downstairs.

"Yup, me."

"This was where it happened?"

"Yup, we didn't have any life lines then. I fell from way up here and when I hit the water I sank to the bottom, dissolving on the way down. That was the last time Captain Nimbo came to gather these lights."

Joe took the harnesses off the hooks. "Here,

slip this over your head." He tugged on the strong nylon straps to make sure they fit the boy snugly. Reaching behind him, Joe grabbed a clamp attached to a sturdy elastic rope and clipped it on the back of Donald's harness. Getting into his own extra-extra large harness, the mudman bent down and requested, "Now, please hook me up to this rope, Donald."

The boy laughed. "I feel like a two-legged dog on a long leash."

"You look like it too, except you're missing a tail," Joe chuckled. He pulled on the harness to make sure it was hooked tightly. "If we fall, we won't fall too far! That was a real high dive I took last time!"

They moved to the stern of the boat and Joe unscrewed one of the round metal covers mounted in the wooden decking. Underneath was a hole about the size of a small dessert plate. "There are thirty of these holes and we need to find the long vacuum hoses that screw into them," Joe explained.

"So that's what the captain was talking about." Donald peered into the hole, wondering how this machine worked.

"Yup. Now where would he have stored those hoses?"

They searched through large closets and big storage spaces, finding bits and pieces of many of the captain's half-completed inventions. Eventually they found a big pile of lengthy, flexible hoses dumped in a back room. They untangled them carefully and crawled from outlet to outlet, attaching each one. When they were finished, there were thirty hoses spread out on the deck at the back of the ferryboat, connected to an unseen machine.

"How does this thing work?" the boy inquired.

"Does it work? That's the question. None of this equipment has been used since I've been gone. Let's check it out," Joe suggested.

Eager to see the big vacuum in action, Donald asked, "What can I do?"

Joe pointed at the wall, "See that line of switches over there . . . yeah, those. Each one operates a vacuum hose. When I give you a thumbs-up signal, like this . . . , " Joe curled in his fat fingers and stuck his big thumb in the air, "it means turn on the next switch. Thumbs-down, means turn it off. OK?"

Donald gave him a thumbs-up signal. "Got it."

Joe handed him a pair of ear plugs and put a large set in his own big ears. Then he turned his thumb up and the boy flipped on the first switch. A machine underneath the deck roared to life, sounding like his mother's vacuum cleaner, but louder. Joe crept on his hands and knees, inspecting each hose for clogs before signaling Donald to throw the next switch. It got noisier every time the boy turned on another vacuum. When all the switches were on, Joe smiled broadly, pleased that the old machine worked perfectly. Without delay, he gave a series of thumbs-down signals to his helpmate who shut off all the switches. "I can't believe it works so well after all this time," Joe marveled. "Let's go tell the captain." They removed their earplugs and climbed the stairs to the pilot house.

"Sounds like the old light-sucker will still do its job," Captain Nimbo commented as they came through the door.

"Yup, it started right up," Joe said with relief.

Captain Nimbo lit his pipe and smoked it contentedly as they journeyed through the dark northern sky. "Well, mates, we're on course and we'll be there in twenty minutes. Have a seat and relax for a bit."

Donald spotted a glow of light far ahead and asked, "What's that?"

Joe smiled, "That's them. Yup, it is. Those are the northern lights—scientifically known as the aurora borealis. Wait till you see them up close."

Smoke arose from Captain Nimbo's pipe as he explained, "The scientists aren't quite sure, but they think these lights occur when the sun's radiation hits the rare gases that are high in the sky. You only find them near the North or South Poles, where you've got a lot of magnetic pull. There's usually a mammoth sunspot just before they appear."

Donald watched the thin curtains of flickering light come into view—ghostly pastel colors of green, yellow and pink. The boy commented, "They're like big neon signs moving in the fog."

Before reducing the power Captain Nimbo

warned, "Buckle up again, mates, and hang on." They were forced forward in their seats as the Flying Ferry Boat slowed down. When she returned to normal speed, the captain asked, "Are you ready to capture some lights, Joe?"

"Aye, aye, Captain. The hoses are all hooked up, but I could use Donald's help again."

"Then go suck up as many as you can, mates." Once again the clumsy mudman stumbled down the steps to the big auto deck. Donald followed close behind.

In a few moments Captain Nimbo's voice called from the intercom, "Attention, mates. Get ready. We're entering the northern lights!" While the boat moved at a leisurely pace, Donald and Joe reattached themselves to the life lines. Watching from the back of the lower deck, Donald stared at the Arctic sky as the pastel colors surrounded them like sheer veils of the softest silk. The Flying Ferry Boat moved through layer after layer of the shimmering lights. The misty colors were in constant motion, making new gauzy shapes every minute or so. Donald was fascinated.

"We're the light catchers tonight, and I think we're going to catch some beauties," Joe said enthusiastically.

Donald shivered in the freezing air. "How many can we get?"

"As many as we can. Put your ear plugs in and let's get to work." He grabbed a hose and cast the open end into the northern lights. "OK, turn on the switch," Joe commanded, giving a

144

quick thumbs-up signal.

Donald flipped on the first switch and a vacuum rumbled into action, sucking in a section of filmy colors. Joe moved the hose back and forth, pulling in streamer after streamer of glowing lights. Then he moved to the next vacuum, gave a thumbs-up signal to his helper and slowly filled that hose. One by one, he diligently moved down the whole row. Eventually a stream of shimmering rays trailed from behind the Flying Ferry Boat. When all the motors were roaring and the vacuum tubes were crammed full, Joe motioned for Donald to join him. Together they proudly admired their hard work.

Donald jumped around and cheered, "Wow! Look at this! Wow! This is incredible!" The sight truly was amazing. The enchanted boy leaned over the edge of the boat to get a better look at the ribbons of light. An especially colorful one caught his eye and he bent over on tiptoes for a closer look.

Suddenly he lost his balance and toppled forward. Without a railing to stop him, he fell overboard and plunged into the northern lights screaming, "H-e-e-e-e-lp! O-o-o-o-h, Joe. Help me!"

The life line stopped his fall. *Boing, boing, boing.* He bounced up and down in the freezing night sky with the spectacular aurora surrounding him. "Stop, Captain. Man overboard!" Joe shouted. "Hang on, Donald, I'll pull you up." Neither Captain Nimbo nor Donald

145

could hear Joe above the noise of the vacuums.

As the ferryboat sped through the muted colors, Donald felt completely alone. Shaking with fear and shivering with cold, he bounced helplessly in the icy Arctic air. His stomach was flip-flopping from the up-and-down motion. The boy couldn't feel Joe pulling up on the elastic life line, so he was surprised to see the hull of the ferryboat coming into view. He was very relieved when Joe's strong arms lifted him on to the deck.

Sobbing, Donald clung to his big friend, feeling the warmth of Joe's body. He trembled as he choked out the words. "Oh, Joe, I thought I was a goner. Now I know how you fell out. My legs are shaking so badly that I can't stand up."

Joe shouted, "I can't hear you. Just take it easy. Take it easy." He unfastened the harnesses, gently lifted Donald into his arms and carried him slowly up the stairs.

Away from the vacuum noise, they took out their ear plugs and could hear each other again. "Thanks for saving me," Donald said, sinking into the mudman's soft arms.

Joe gave him a hug. "Yup. No problem. Good thing you had on a life line."

"Yeah, I know," Donald sighed. "That was really scary, Joe. I hope the captain doesn't know I fell out. He didn't want me to be a bunch of trouble."

Still holding the boy in his arms, Joe 'Dobe quietly answered, "I doubt if he heard anything above the noise of the vacuums. See how quickly an accident can happen? Now we both know the importance of safety belts."

When they reached the living quarters Donald requested, "Please put me down. I think I can make it on my own now." He lightheartedly wondered, "Do you think anyone else has gone bungee jumping into the aurora borealis?"

"Nope," Joe chuckled, "you're probably the first."

They took the stairs to the pilot house two at a time, startling the captain as they burst into the small room. "We've caught some lights, more than I ever caught alone," Joe said. "I can't wait to decorate San Francisco."

Donald opened his small hand and gently blew on the floating light rays he'd been hiding in his closed fist. The faint colors scattered around the pilot house and attached themselves to the metal surfaces. A soft glow filled the little room.

"You should see our tail of lights, Captain," the boy exclaimed. "I'll bet we look like a giant comet."

"Well, mate, I've heard of the Star Ship, but I've never heard of the Comet Ship," the captain replied.

"Yup, we're riding in the Comet Ship," Joe laughed.

Excited, Donald declared, "Let's have a party! I'll make the popcorn. OK, you guys?"

"I could do with a small celebration myself," Captain Nimbo agreed. "Let me get the ship back at rocket speed before you start cooking,

Donald. Buckle up, mates! Here we go again!"

The Flying Ferry Boat jerked forward, throwing them against the back of their seats. She sped through the darkness toward San Francisco. The glowing tail of delicate lights swirled behind them.

Munching on popcorn and sipping sodas, they relaxed, leaving the dark Arctic sky behind as they flew south into the California sunshine. After some time, Captain Nimbo slowed the ship to normal speed and announced, "Attention, mates, we're almost back to San Francisco. I can see the lighthouse at Point Reyes just ahead of us.

"Before we decorate the City, I want to make a quick flight around the Bay and treat the cleanup crews to the amazing spectacle of the Comet Ship. We'll have a one-boat parade in the sky." The captain lowered their altitude and turned inland, guiding the Flying Ferry Boat between the tall towers of the famous Golden Gate Bridge.

Donald took in the views on either side of him. Looking north, he saw Alcatraz still surrounded by mud. To the south, he could see Pier 39 and the tall downtown skyscrapers. He also noticed the tankers, cruise ships and sailboats tilted on the mud beside their docks. They continued parading past Candlestick Park and over the airport always keeping the sea of brown mud on their left and the crowded freeways and house-filled hillsides on their right.

The cleanup crews were finishing their work

along the shoreline when the Flying Ferry Boat appeared overhead. The three-storied white boat flew slowly, with its amazing rainbow tail of lights swirling from the stern. Donald and Joe waved to the children from the side windows. Now and then Captain Nimbo sounded the massive air horn, *boooomp*, making sure everyone noticed them.

Piles of bright orange bags were stacked along the shore as far as Donald could see. They looked like an immense fluorescent ribbon wrapping the Bay. Donald happily cried, "Wow! This *is* a big, cleanup project—way bigger than I thought."

Joe smiled his broadest smile. "Yup, it sure is. The sea life is going to have a cleaner place to live in now."

At the southern tip of the mud, the captain turned the flying ship and made a wide circle over Silicon Valley. Then they headed north along the opposite side of the Bay. In time they crossed over the lengthy Oakland-Bay Bridge. The uncovered BART tube lay next to it, snaking across the mud. Finally the captain made a wide horseshoe turn around San Pablo Bay.

The parade ended when the Flying Ferry Boat came to a sudden stop in midair, hovering over the northern tower of the Golden Gate Bridge. "The show is over. It's time to go to work, mates," the captain announced. "You know what to do, right Joe?"

"Yup, I do! You come with me, Donald." On their way downstairs the mudman explained,

"Putting lights on this bridge will be our first job. These veils of color will stick to whatever metal objects they touch, like they did in the pilot house."

"How long will they last?" Donald inquired.

"At least through New Year's Eve."

They put in their ear plugs and reattached themselves to the life lines. Using hand signals, Donald again operated the switches. Joe squatted beside the first vacuum tube and gave a thumbs-down sign. When Donald shut off the vacuum, the delicate lights fell from the hose and immediately attached themselves to the metal on the orange bridge. Joe shook the tube gently to get out all the lights. The boat moved, hovered, then moved again as Joe emptied each one. When he was finished, the Golden Gate Bridge shimmered.

They decorated the bigger buildings and famous landmarks in the City, one after another. The cleanup workers close by watched the softly glowing lights as they dropped slowly from the stern of the ferryboat. The pastel lights added a colorful polish to the window frames, antennas, railings and even to the cars that happened to pass under them. One cable car near Ghirardelli Square received a sprinkling of colors. It gleamed as it traveled through the city streets, up and down the steep hills. Little by little the City changed into a magical place.

They put the last light ribbon on Sutro Tower, the huge microwave tower standing like a sentinel above the San Francisco. Then the vacuums were silent again. Joe and Donald took out their ear plugs and gazed below as the wisps of color danced in the breeze.

Captain Nimbo praised his crew as the Flying Ferry Boat soared above the decorated city toward Crissy Field. "Those lights glow like a rainbow over the Pacific. Well done, mates."

"Yup, Merry Christmas San Francisco!"

"Awesome!

Suggested Activity: *Go to the Exploratorium at the historic Palace of Fine Arts located at Marina Blvd. and Lyon. Play with the light exhibits. Phone: 415-561-0360.*

Chapter 11

Hey, We Cleaned Up the Bay!

It was late afternoon. The sun had dropped below the high clouds and inched slowly toward the horizon. The cleanup crews at Crissy Field piled the last of the bags full of trash on shore and the tiny crabs scurried back to their homes. The muddy workers found water faucets and began washing their hands and faces. They also scraped some of the mud from their shoes and clothes. Camera crews, stage hands and city officials were busy preparing for the big party.

The ferryboat came toward them, flying at a very low altitude. Her colorful tail of lights was gone, so she no longer looked like a comet ship. Everyone wondered why the boat was not landing on the old runway.

Captain Nimbo called over the intercom to his crew, "Attention mates! It's time to pick up the plug and put it back into place. Get ready for the hookup, Joe."

"Aye, aye, Captain!" the mudman answered in a cheerful voice. The boat hovered over the huge round of concrete. "Donald, stand up front," Joe ordered. "Guide the captain into position."

The youngest crew member moved forward on the auto deck, keeping one eye on the loop of the plug and the other eye on the captain standing in the pilot house. He hand-signaled right, left, up or down until they were above the loop. At that point Donald waved a big OK by putting his thumb and forefinger together and flashed a big smile up at the captain.

Joe 'Dobe pushed the hook into position and quickly snagged the loop. "OK, we got her," he bellowed, motioning for the captain to pull up.

The Flying Ferry Boat gained altitude, lifting the huge plug into the air. They flew over the heads of the gathering crowd and across the sea of mud. The captain stopped above the drain and waited for the giant plug to quit swinging. Then he carefully centered it, dropped his altitude and plugged the hole.

"Well, that was sure easy," Joe said as he released the hook.

The captain's voice came through the speaker congratulating his capable crew. "Well done, mates! Now we're off to the cleanup party!" He turned the big boat around, headed back to Crissy Field and carefully landed.

By now a swift breeze was blowing in from the ocean and the sun was creating long shadows on the ground. After Captain Nimbo shut down the engines, a worrisome thought passed through his mind and he called below, "Did either of you see King Crab anywhere?"

"Nope," they sadly answered in unison.

The captain stroked his beard, commenting unhappily, "Oh, fish! I was hoping he'd show up by now." He shrugged his shoulders, adjusted his hat and went below to join his crew. A happy cluster of children gathered around the Flying Ferry Boat and a high school band began to play as Captain Nimbo, Joe 'Dobe and Donald climbed down the ladder. All of them formed an impromptu parade and marched noisily down the asphalt to the party.

There was much activity at the old air base. Buses arrived from points all around the Bay to drop off their crews of muddy workers. Trash trucks picked up the piles of plastic bags and hauled them away to the landfill areas. A car with a shiny new yellow kayak strapped on top pulled into the almost full parking lot. And the mayor arrived to lead the celebration.

Brightly colored nylon flags and bouquets of balloons hung above the portable stage along with a colorful banner that read *Hey, We Cleaned Up the Bay!* Orange bags full of trash were stacked across the back of the platform and a huge number of people were gathering on the grass, waiting for things to begin. When the tiny parade passed through the crowd, the children pointed at Donald and whispered among themselves.

"That's the boy who built the mudman."

"His name is Donald."

"He's not very old, is he?"

"I wish I could ride on the ferryboat like he

did."

A reporter suddenly stuck a microphone in Donald's face and asked him about pulling the plug. Overwhelmed by all the attention, the young boy didn't know what to say, so he tugged on Joe's hand. The mudman smiled down at the reporter and then said the same thing over and over, "Yup, we did it. Yup, we did it once again."

The mayor climbed the steps to the platform to begin the festivities. He held his hands up to quiet the crowd. When he had everyone's attention, he spoke. "Thank you all for coming to this *Hey, We Cleaned Up the Bay!* party. As you know, lots of trash has been dumped into the Bay over the years." The mayor gestured to the crowd. "I want to thank you children, teachers, parents, truck and bus drivers. This cleanup couldn't have happened without you. Give yourselves a big hand!" The people clapped, shouting and whistling as well.

"I'd like to honor three special people this evening: Captain Nimbo, Joe 'Dobe and Donald Jordan. Gentlemen, will you please join me here on the stage?" The crowd cheered while the band struck up a tune and followed the crew on to the platform. A television camera zoomed in to film the ferryboat crew and the reporters began making notes for their news reports.

Clearing his throat, the mayor continued, "At one time San Francisco Bay was beautiful and unpolluted. That was because Captain Nimbo and Joe 'Dobe, using the Flying Ferry Boat, would pull the plug and drain the dirty

water out of the Bay. King Crab, king of the sea life, would then command the smaller crabs to eat the green ring of algae growing around the edge. When the Bay was refilled with new sea water, it would sparkle once again.

"Then many years ago on a trip to the North Pole, Joe 'Dobe accidentally fell into the Arctic Ocean and disappeared. Since he was no longer here to help Captain Nimbo, the dirty water has not been drained for years."

The mayor moved to Donald's side and placed a hand on his shoulder. "After our recent earthquake, this fine young man, Donald Jordan, somehow rebuilt Joe 'Dobe. Of course he had no idea that he was recreating a famous mudman. When Joe 'Dobe came to life, he brought the boy on this adventure. The captain told me that Donald has proved to be a very useful crew member on the Flying Ferry Boat." The young mate straightened his shoulders and smiled proudly.

"Captain Nimbo, Joe 'Dobe and Donald Jordan, I have a special award for you. As mayor of the City of San Francisco, I present you each with a key to the City." The mayor shook their hands and smiled. "We thank you for making our Bay a cleaner place." While the audience applauded, he turned to Captain Nimbo and offered him the microphone.

The skinny captain put his hands on his hips and barked, "When are landlubbers going to learn? If everyone would put their trash in the trash cans, it wouldn't end up in the water.

I can't be emptying the Bay every week or two, so please pick up after yourselves. That would keep the whole Bay shipshape and the crabs would be less crabby." The cleanup workers clapped politely.

Then the mayor turned to Donald. "I understand you have something you want to say."

"Yes, I do," he gulped. The man lowered the microphone to the boy's level. Feeling nervous, Donald tried to speak clearly, "The Bay is clean, but now we're all dirty. Moms and dads, when your bathtubs and towels get muddy tonight, please don't be upset. They'll clean up, just like the Bay did!"

"Good point, Donald," the mayor remarked.

The parents clapped and nodded their approval. All of the children cheered for Donald.

Surprising even himself, Joe stepped up and spoke in his deep voice. "I'm glad to be back. Yup, I am. But now King Crab is missing. I'm really worried because we haven't seen him since we pulled the plug." Feeling very sad, Joe stepped back heavily from the microphone.

Then the mayor said, "Like Joe just said, we're quite concerned. We're not sure what happened to this king of the sea life."

Suddenly Donald began jumping up and down, pointing toward the back of the crowd. "It's King Crab! It's King Crab!" he yelled.

A demanding voice ordered, "Make way for the king! Step aside! Get out of my way!"

Joe and the captain elbowed each other, relieved to see the king. The crowd moved apart to make a pathway for the gigantic crustacean who wore a splendid crown. With great respect the mayor bowed and the workers removed their hats.

King Crab moved sideways toward the platform, dragging a pile of smelly junk. He was followed by four children carrying orange bags full of more stinking stuff. People held their noses and quietly said things like *Yuk!* or *Ugh!* or *What a stink!* when he passed them.

Awkwardly lifting himself on to the stage, the big crab commented, "I want you to see what we have to deal with in our underwater homes." Then he dumped a rusted car fender, two worn tires, a filthy plastic bucket, a moldy chair cushion and some bent aluminum window frames on the ground in front of the stage. Following his example, the children emptied their bags on the pile—cans, bottles, disposable diapers, rotted old shoes and foul smelling rubbish of every kind and description.

The mayor attempted to smile, but really wanted to hold his nose. Not only did the junk have a terrible odor, but the crab himself smelled like a bottle of fish perfume. Swallowing and taking a deep breath to regain his composure, the leader of the City greeted the king. "I am pleased to meet you, Your Majesty. I'm really glad you're here. I have heard about you for years and I understand you rule the underwater creatures with fairness and diplomacy."

Placing the key to the City in the king's claw, the mayor proclaimed, "It's my honor to present this to you. I truly appreciate the efforts of your many crab subjects in cleaning up San Francisco Bay. It is a shock to see some of the trash that was dumped into your home. I hope we can learn the importance of keeping our bay clean." The mayor stepped back while the audience applauded.

Adjusting his crown and standing up to his full height, King Crab waved his bejeweled claw over the crowd, commanding their attention. "We underwater creatures deserve your respect. We don't throw litter into your homes, so please stop throwing it into ours. Do you realize that a whole generation of crabs, and people for that matter, have never seen how clear and sparkling our bay water can be? Today, with team effort, we start anew. I thank you all for making this day possible." King Crab extended his mammoth pincer to the mayor. A television camera zoomed in to get a close-up shot of them shaking hand and claw. The audience cheered and clapped loudly. They all left the stage while the band played another lively tune.

With the program over, a news photographer asked the ferryboat crew, "Could you three please pose with King Crab? I'd like to get a group picture with this disgusting pile of trash."

Joe 'Dobe and Captain Nimbo stood on either side of King Crab. Donald sat on one of the king's bent claws. As the cameras flashed, Donald whispered, "Where have you been? We thought you went down the drain."

Straightening his bow tie, the king answered,

"I almost did, but fortunately I got caught in a tangle of cable. The water whooshed and whirled around me for many hours, but somehow I survived. It took me most of today to free myself." He frowned as he looked toward the captain, then scowled, "I intend to talk to Nimbo about this. He pulled the plug on me."

Just then Grani Ann came forward wearing a new blue hat. She presented bouquets of flowers to her rescuers and gave each of them a kiss and another thank you.

The crowd surrounded them, eager to shake their hands. "Donald," a familiar voice called. "Donald! Hey, Donald!"

The boy was surprised to hear his mother's voice. "Mom? Is that you?"

"I'm over here!" she called, waving wildly. "Dad's here, too!" Donald stood on tiptoes and searched for the faces of his parents among the sea of heads. It took him a minute to spot them because they were as muddy as everyone else.

The boy called, "Hi, Mom! Hi, Dad!" Glad to see his parents, Donald pushed his way through the workers to greet them. He showed them his key to the City and the gold coin from King Crab. He felt very important.

His dad patted him on the back. "We're so proud of you, son."

"Yes, we sure are," his mother quickly added, wrapping her arms around him. "But I was worried. I don't like you being with people we don't know."

Donald replied gently, "I'm fine, Mom. Besides, you met Joe 'Dobe before he came to life. And I'm learning a lot from Captain Nimbo."

"We think you should come home with us," his father stated firmly.

"Dad, I'm ten years old and I really want to stay with Joe and the captain a while longer. Please!" he pleaded.

Looking the boy in the eye, his dad seemed to understand. "Okay, son, but not for too much longer."

Donald's mom surprisingly agreed. "I can see you're having a great adventure, but do come home soon. I miss you, you know."

At that moment, Donald spotted Captain Nimbo heading for the ferryboat. Leaving Joe 'Dobe and King Crab to shake hands with the workers, he quickly kissed his parents good-bye and ran to catch up with the captain. "What's up?" the boy asked.

"Enough of this hoopla. It's time to open the gate and let the sea water back in."

The two of them hurried on to the ferryboat and made their way to the pilot house. Sitting at his desk, the captain checked his Mebus 21. It showed the closed gate on the computer screen. He immediately sent a radio warning to the ships waiting to enter the Bay. The message was: *Secure your anchors. The gate will be opening soon and the water currents will be dangerous.*

As the sun moved to the horizon, Captain Nimbo sounded the ferryboat horn to quiet the crowd, *boooomp, boooomp.* Following the captain's instructions, the mayor returned to the microphone and made one last statement. "Please move to the beach and look beneath the Bridge. Captain Nimbo says there is a spectacular sight in store for us."

Back on the ferryboat the captain said, "The mayor just made his announcement, so it's time to let in the clean water. The coast is clear. Do you want to push the button, Donald?"

Donald shouted an enthusiastic, "Yes!"

"OK, mate, push the OPEN GATE button."

"Aye, aye, Captain."

They turned to watch the image on the computer screen as the golden dam began moving steadily downward. Captain Nimbo sounded three triumphant blasts on the ferryboat horn, *boooomp, boooomp, boooomp.* Then he suggested, "Come on, Donald, let's go watch this with Joe and King Crab and everyone else."

When they reached the beach, they easily spotted Joe 'Dobe's head towering above the adults. His voice boomed out, "Keep watching, folks. It's going to happen soon." As Donald and the captain reached his side, they heard murmurs of amazement going through the crowd.

"Look at that. The gold gate is going down."

"Hey! Some water is coming over the top."

"It's a little waterfall."

"But it's getting bigger."

"What's that roar?"

"What's that rumble?"

"It sounds like a freight train."

"Oh, my gosh!"

"It's a real waterfall."

"...like Niagara Falls."

"Wow!"

"So that's what you were talking about—the golden gate waterfall," Donald declared. "It's just awesome!"

"Yup," Joe said proudly.

Sea water gushed over the top of the descending gate and crashed in a thunderous cascade on to the muddy floor of the Bay. A fine mist sprayed from the falls. When the gate dropped all the way down, the waterfall disappeared and the ocean water flowed easily through the narrow opening. It quickly filled the Bay, bringing fish and other sea life with it.

At the same time, a brilliant orange and pink sunset spread across the sky. The remaining sunlight reflected on the feathery clouds overhead and the puffy white clouds that were blowing in from offshore. In the twilight the vivid colors were mirrored on the sparkling water. It was a sight to remember.

After the sunset faded, the pastel streamers of northern lights glowed softly on the graceful spans of the bridge. "Look! The buildings have those lights, too," a child noticed.

Hearing her, Joe 'Dobe's mouth turned up with the biggest smile ever. "Yup, we lit up all of San Francisco! Captain Nimbo and I used to do this at Christmas time before there were lighted decorations."

It had been an unforgettable evening, but now it was completely dark. The cold wind was blowing even harder. The mayor said good-bye, the reporters left, families hurried to their cars and the teachers led their students on to the waiting school buses.

Pulling his hat down tightly, Captain Nimbo said, "Let's shove off, mates. I want to fly to Twin Peaks and look at the northern lights from up there. We can even spend the night and watch the sun rise over the Bay. Do you want to come with us, King?"

"No. I've been away from my grotto for too long already. I need to check on my subjects." The giant crab gave a quick wave with his claw and began to scuttle sideways toward the clean water.

Captain Nimbo barked, "Not so fast, King. Aren't you going to shake my hand and tell me thanks."

King Crab grandly swung his claw about and fumed, "Thanks for what, Captain? For pulling the plug on me when I was under the water?"

Captain Nimbo looked at the ground sheepishly and shuffled his feet. When he didn't answer, Joe awkwardly said, "We were all worried about you . . . and we did look for you . . . and we're glad you didn't go down the drain."

Captain Nimbo nodded his head, not knowing what to say. After another moment of dead silence, he finally spoke, "I'm sorry, Your Majesty. I won't do it again, sea dog's honor."

King Crab royally accepted his apology and extended his giant claw in friendship. With the conflict over, they all congratulated each other and said their good-byes.

The crew of three boarded the ferryboat. Captain Nimbo radioed the anchored boats to let them know that it was now safe to enter the Bay. Donald pulled the cord to give a long blast on the big horn, *boooomp*. Joe 'Dobe called in his deep voice, "Clear the runway."

Suggested Activity: *Help keep San Francisco clean by picking up one piece of trash every day. Encourage everyone in your group to do this. If you should see the little crabs eating algae off the rocks, please let them do their work.*

Chapter 12

Farewell to Joe 'Dobe

The Flying Ferry Boat took off into the wind, soaring above the glowing city. It was a quick flight to the matching hilltops high above Market Street. Captain Nimbo knew that Twin Peaks was the best place in San Francisco for a view of the City. He carefully dropped the ferryboat down at one end of the parking lot and turned off the engine. The crew left the boat and joined the other people who had come to look at the night scene. It was spectacular with the additional glow of the northern lights.

Donald shivered when the icy blasts of wind hit him, but he was too excited to pay much attention to the cold. "Can I climb that little peak?" he inquired, pointing behind him.

"You sure can," Captain Nimbo replied. "You get almost a 360 degree view of San Francisco from up there. During the day you can even see the Pacific Ocean."

Donald tucked his hands under his arms to keep them warm. "Would you go up there with me, Joe?"

"Yup, why not. Let's all go."

Donald was so certain the answer would be *yup* that he was already running toward the treeless hill. He carefully crossed the road and hurried up the well-worn path. When he reached the top, he leaned into the howling wind and struggled to stand upright. It was several minutes before Joe and Captain Nimbo arrived.

"Wow!" the boy exclaimed after he had turned around several times. "This is some view—and the lights look great, Joe."

"Yup, they're pretty special all right," Joe commented.

"I want my parents to see this sometime. How do we get here?" Donald asked.

The captain answered, "Just follow your nose to Sutro Tower. It's the tallest structure in San Francisco and you can see it from all directions. Then look for these two little peaks close by."

"That's easy enough," Donald replied, holding on to his hat to keep it from blowing away. At the same time, he pointed to the other peak and asked, "Can we climb that one now?"

"Sure," Captain Nimbo answered. "We're not on any schedule tonight."

"Come on, Joe, let's race!" Donald called.

"I'm coming and I can take a lot bigger steps than you can!" Joe yelled, accepting the challenge. They hurried down the dirt path, jumping from the timbered stairs that held the soil in place. The three friends raced through the darkness, stumbling and tripping down one hillside, across the road and up the steps to the second peak. Donald and Joe reached the top in a tied race. Captain Nimbo arrived seconds later. All three of them were out of breath and sweating in the cold night air. None of them noticed the big gray clouds above them, moving in from the ocean.

"For your size, you're really fast, Joe," Donald said.

"Yup, you usually don't see mud move so quickly," Joe acknowledged. "I've had to race raindrops all my life, so I'm in fairly good shape. And this chocolate foot works as well as the mud one."

They stood together admiring the view from the second peak, unaware that a tremendous storm was rapidly brewing. The wind whistled in their ears and soon a misty rain dampened the ground, but they were too caught up in the aftermath of the race to consider the warning.

Craaaack!! A bolt of lightening cut through the sky, striking the tall tower nearby. *Boooom!* Thunder crashed, then large drops of rain beat down on them.

"Oh, no! I'm getting wet!" Joe yelped.

The captain quickly handed Joe his hat. "Here, put this on." *Splaaaash!! Splaaaash!!* The sky suddenly dumped buckets of water, drenching them in seconds. Captain Nimbo hollered, "Blasted barnacles! Let's get back to the boat."

With every step, the unexpected downpour washed another layer of adobe off Joe's body. The toes of his mud foot quickly softened and fell off. Captain Nimbo and Donald each grabbed a hand, attempting to help him as he limped down the steep steps. However, Joe's muddy fingers were so squishy that they fell apart as soon as they were touched. Soon the rest of his gooey hands dropped off at the wrists. As the deluge continued, Donald yelled frantically, "Hurry, Joe! Run! We've got to get you out of this rain."

The hat protected the top of the mudman's large head, but his nose, lips and chin were pelted with water and rapidly disappeared. Joe stuttered, "I'm . . . I'm . . . w--washing a--way."

As his adobe body softened, large hunks of mud began coming loose. Water mixed with mud ran down the sides of his face, destroying his ears and making his neck weaker and weaker. His head fell forward so he could no longer see where he was going.

Donald cried, "We've got to do something fast!"

". . . Yup," Joe cried faintly. Every time they pushed or pulled or tried to guide him, more of the mushy mud fell off. Sheets of rain were whipped in every direction by the wind. The water washed away layers of mud from his arms, legs and torso. Joe 'Dobe became thinner and thinner. He staggered on as thunder and lightening hit around them. His chocolate foot loosened and came off. By this time his legs were so thin that they could no longer support his body and he collapsed on the ground. As he fell, his head gooshed into the earth. *Splaaaat!*

The mudman said nothing more.

Donald's panic turned into tears and anger at the rain pouring from the sky. He shook his fist at the raindrops and wailed, "Stop! Stop, you stupid storm!! See what you've done! You've destroyed my friend!"

Captain Nimbo was terribly upset to see Joe erode right before his eyes. "Donald, maybe we can save what's left of him. Let's roll his body to the ferryboat."

They gently began to roll the remains of Joe's torso down the hill. Unfortunately, the huge mud mass gained speed and soon plunged ahead of them into the darkness. "Joe! Joe! Wait for us! Please stop!!" Donald cried, chasing after him. But Joe didn't stop. The big rolling mudball careened down the hill and squashed on the street. Then it slid away into the shrubbery on the steep slope below.

"What an idiot I am! Rolling him was a big mistake," Captain Nimbo admitted, angry with himself. "Joe 'Dobe is gone again."

The storm raged, pulling the warmth from their bodies and filling their shoes with water. They stood together on the hillside. Donald was crying salty tears that mixed with the rain water and streamed down his cheeks. He sobbed, "I built Joe and now he's gone. I wish we'd never raced to the second peak. Oh, Captain, what can I do?"

Captain Nimbo spoke honestly, "Well, you can cry until the fish stop swimming, but he's certainly not going to come back to life right now."

Just then Donald remembered, "His chocolate foot should be somewhere. It might still be in one piece." They carefully retraced their steps up the slippery slope, searching for the pillow-sized hunk of candy. A well-timed flash of lightening helped them locate the foot. "There it is, Captain."

"I'll get it." Captain Nimbo solemnly lifted the sticky chocolate off the ground, cradling it in his arms. "This is beginning to soften too, just not as fast as the mud."

Donald was shivering from top to bottom when he spotted the captain's muddy cap. As he picked it up, he moaned, "I'm so cold I can't feel my fingers anymore!"

"Let's go, mate. We certainly don't need hypothermia tonight." The captain led the boy down the washed out pathway. "We might be soaked to the skin, but at least we're waterproof."

"When I build Joe 'Dobe again, I'll figure out a way to waterproof him," Donald said with determination, wiping his nose on his sleeve. "Maybe I'll make him completely out of chocolate next time, or add something to the mud to make it hold together better."

"Unfortunately, that might be a problem, mate. I'll tell you more after we get inside." They hurried along the road and finally climbed the ladder into the welcome shelter of the ferryboat. They left muddy footprints on the stairs as they slogged up to the living quarters.

The captain laid the softened chocolate foot on the big table. He took off his wet shoes and socks and went to his cabin to get some dry clothes for both of them. While he was there, he peeled off his dripping shirt and slipped into his moth-eaten robe. On his way to the galley to fix something hot to drink, he told Donald to go take a warm shower.

The numb boy followed orders. He pulled his treasured coin from King Crab out of his pocket and carefully placed it on the table. He heaped his soggy clothes in a pile and hurried into the bathroom. Donald was shaking with cold as he turned on the water and waited for it to heat. After he stepped under the warm water, he stood there for a long time, crying and thinking about building Joe 'Dobe again. When he was completely warm, he got out, dried off and put on Captain Nimbo's long pants and baggy sweat shirt.

Waddling into the galley, Donald found a large mug of hot chocolate sitting on the counter for him. The captain was sipping a cup of steaming coffee. Clouds of smoke rose from his pipe as he remarked, "What a terrible way to end your adventure."

"Yeah, it is," Donald agreed, blowing on his hot cocoa.

"I mixed up some pancake batter," Captain Nimbo said gently. "I was hungry and thought some solid food might be good for us."

"I do like pancakes," Donald said. "Why don't you go take your shower, Captain? I'll cook them."

"Thanks, I'll take you up on that. I'm cold as a starfish." The captain quietly left the room.

Donald sipped his hot chocolate, feeling lonely and unhappy. When he thought about Joe's strong hand and jolly laugh, his shoulders drooped and the tears flooded down his cheeks. After a time, he poured some batter into the hot skillet and started cooking. He felt sad again when he set only two places at the table.

Coming back into the galley after his shower, Captain Nimbo said quietly, "Joe would want to eat if he were here, so let's have some grub."

Donald handed him a plate of hot pancakes. "The butter and syrup are on the table. Do you want more coffee?"

Downhearted, the captain pulled himself up to the table and began buttering his hot cakes. They ate their meal in silence, each thinking their own thoughts.

Later, over a second cup of coffee, the captain lit his pipe and started a conversation. "It hardly seems possible that you are the green sea boy who came on board three days ago. You learned to follow my orders, you came through when we had emergencies and you just cooked the pancakes. You've even learned to get along with me. I guess you're following in Joe's footsteps and becoming my second mate."

"Yeah, I think I've grown up a little bit," Donald acknowledged. "Besides, I like being part of the crew."

The captain praised his small mate. "I have

to say, you are one of the finest young landlubbers ever to set foot on my boat. You can come work with me anytime."

Donald smiled briefly at Captain Nimbo, then thoughtfully said, "Captain, I think I'm ready to go home now. I know my mom really misses me."

"I can fly you back any time."

"The sooner I get home, the sooner I can start building Joe again," Donald explained.

"Well, you can make another mudman, but he probably won't turn into Joe 'Dobe."

Donald raised his eyebrows and looked Captain Nimbo in the eye. "What?! Why not?"

"I don't really know." Captain Nimbo went on to explain, "You see, when you finished him the right energy was there to bring him to life, but it isn't there all the time. It seems to take a special person, the right mud mixture and some unusual chain of events for him to exist. I tried over and over to rebuild him after he fell overboard. My mudmen just sat there day after day, never breathing or taking a step, and I finally gave up."

Amazed, Donald exclaimed, "Wow! What did I do?"

"Maybe the earthquake shook some life into that mud you used. If I knew the answer for sure, we could rebuild him together."

"Will I ever see him again?"

"Probably so," the captain replied.

"So you think someone else might build him?" Donald asked.

"That's right," the captain answered. "Somehow. Somewhere. Sometime. You did it and someone did it before you. I just know that he's never been rebuilt by the same person or in exactly the same place. That's what I've been wanting to tell you."

More questions flooded out of Donald's mouth. "But Captain, what if nobody ever tries again? What if he never comes back? What if everyone completely forgets about him?"

"Will you ever forget him?"

"Never."

"Will the people who saw him the past few days forget him?"

"No, they probably won't," Donald brightened. "King Crab remembered and so did all those old guys at Fisherman's Wharf."

"And let me remind you, Donald," Captain Nimbo commented, "the man you built was exactly the same lovable, clumsy guy that I knew before. He even said *yup* and had a big, booming voice. Joe will turn up again. Just you wait and see."

"What are we going to do with his chocolate foot?" Donald asked.

"That's up to you."

Looking at the big hunk of chocolate, the boy easily made a decision. "Could you drop it off at Ghirardelli Square? If Joe ever needs another foot, maybe he'll go there—and this one will be waiting for him."

"What a great idea, mate. I'll take care of that." Captain Nimbo got up from the table and carried the dirty dishes into the galley. "Come on, I'll fly you home. We can be there in less than an hour."

Donald picked up his gold coin and clenched it tightly in his fist. "I'm ready, Captain," he bravely said.

The crew of two headed for the pilot house. Captain Nimbo pulled the cord for the ferryboat horn to announce their departure, *boooomp.* Letting go of his sadness, Donald opened the window and shouted in the biggest voice he could muster, "Clear the runway!"

At they took off into the storm clouds, Donald called out, "Hey, Joe, wherever you are, thanks for the best adventure ever. And thanks for holding my hand!"

Suggested Activity: *Drive to Twin Peaks for a gorgeous view of San Francisco. Then climb both little hills as Donald did. To get there drive west on Market Street, wind carefully into the hills and then, as you start down the other side, look for the Twin Peaks road sign showing you where to turn right.*

Do you have any ideas about
what might happen next ?

Will someone build Joe 'Dobe again?
Who?
Where will they go?
What will they do?
How will they do it?
Why will they do it?
When will this happen?
Who will they meet?
Will there be a Flying Ferry Boat?

Write your comments to:
     Judy Dumm
     P.O. Box 2116
     Santa Rosa, CA 95405-0116

Or E-Mail your ideas to:
     ffboat@sonic.net

You may also visit the **Flying Ferry Boat**
on the web at:
     http://www.sonic.net/flyingferryboat

     (A suggested curriculum for teachers
     is also available at this web site.)

Acknowledgments

Writing this book has definitely been a challenge for me and I want to acknowledge the following people:

First I want to thank my family for remembering the stories. The Jordan children—Donita, Ellen Jane, Jack and Donald, Jr., who all played a part in the original tales. Their children—Judy, Curt and Jack Reynolds; Linelle, Maureen and Robert McDonald; Ken and Amy Jordan. And my daughters, Jennifer and Jill.

Cathy Vertuca gave me vital editing assistance, smoothing out the rough spots and making the story work on paper. The illustrator, Timothy Allen Estrada, brought Joe 'Dobe to life for me, then agreed to draw the rest of the pictures. He also drew the cover art and, with Kristin Burkart's digital expertise, we added color to the cover design. Donita Reynolds, Russell Wilkie, Walter Kent, Jr., Pat Coggins, Marcia Burkart, Patricia Heeb, Debra Sandine, Barbara Shinabargar and Linda Allen all read the manuscript and offered valuable input. Nanci Burton, Judy McAuliffe, Grace Dumm, Linda Simonds, Betty Smith and Ruth Pritchard gave me moral support and good ideas. My parents, Jack and Donita Reynolds, provided the financial assistance so the book could be printed.

Thanks also to Mike Carey, Stephanie Kirk and one of the third grade classes at Pine Crest School in Sebastopol, California. These students listened to my manuscript, drew pictures of the main characters and offered wonderful suggestions. They requested more illustrations and informed me that Captain Nimbo smoked a pipe, of course. I thank them for their interest and enthusiasm which added another push toward making this book happen.

Deep gratitude goes to my daughters Jennifer and Jill for their love and encouragement. Finally, I thank my husband Roger, who provides the strong Joe 'Dobe hand in my life.

ACTIVITY LIST

CHAPTER 1
Get some clay and sculpt a mud person you would like for a friend. Or just try making a great hand to hold. If you are in certain areas of the Santa Cruz Mountains, you will find adobe clay in the ground.

CHAPTER 2
Captain Nimbo uses many sea-going terms. What do you think these terms mean? Look in the dictionary or ask some of the sailors down by the wharf.

CHAPTER 3
Climb aboard the old white ferryboat located at the National Maritime Museum at the Hyde Street Pier near Fisherman's Wharf. Phone: 415-556-3002. Or ride a new ferryboat across the Bay to Sausalito or Tiburon. Phone: 415-546-2628 for information. Phone: 415-546-2700 for ferryboat tickets.

CHAPTER 4
Ride BART to the Merritt Street Station in Oakland. You can catch it underground along Market Street in downtown San Francisco. What is its route under the Bay? How far under the water is the tube? Where is the control center? Phone: 415-992-2278.

CHAPTER 5
Learn about San Francisco Bay by visiting the Bay Model Visitor Center, 2100 Bridgeway in Sausalito. Call ahead for the hours and to see if there is water in the model. Phone: 415-332-3870.

CHAPTER 6
Visit Alcatraz and try to find where you think the entrance to King Crab's grotto might be. Call ahead for reservations and ask for the audio tour. Phone: 415-546-2805 for information. Phone: 415-546-2700 for reservations and tickets.

CHAPTER 7
Go and see the crab cookers at Fisherman's Wharf. Try a bite of crab. While you're there, visit the Boudin Bakery and ride the elevator up to Alioto's restaurant. Then go have a world famous hot fudge sundae at the Ghirardelli Chocolate Manufactory at Ghirardelli Square.

CHAPTER 8
Park at Crissy Field in the Presidio and walk along the sandy shoreline toward the Golden Gate Bridge. Visit Fort Point. Phone: 415-556-1693. If you are really ambitious, follow the steep path up the hillside and walk across the Bridge. The deepest part of the Bay is just to the north of the middle of the Bridge.

CHAPTER 9
Prepare some Raspbannies for breakfast. The recipe is on page 132.

CHAPTER 10
Go to the Exploratorium at the historic Palace of Fine Arts located at Marina Blvd. and Lyon. Play with the light exhibits. Phone: 415-561-0360.

CHAPTER 11
Help keep San Francisco clean by picking up one piece of trash every day. Encourage everyone in your group to do this. If you should see the little crabs eating the algae off the rocks, please let them do their work.

CHAPTER 12
Drive to Twin Peaks for a gorgeous view of San Francisco. Then climb both little hills as Donald did. To get there drive west on Market Street, wind carefully into the hills and then, as you start down the other side, look for the Twin Peaks road sign showing you where to turn right.

Mail Order Form

Please send **The Flying Ferry Boat** to:

Name_____

Address_____

City_____State_____Zip_____

_____@ $6.99   =_____
Quantity

7.5% Sales Tax (Calif. residents)   =_____

Subtotal   =_____

Shipping/Handling*   =_____

Total Enclosed   =[   ]

*Please enclose $4.50 to cover shipping and handling, or $6.00 if ordering 3-5 books.

☐ If you wish to pay by check or money order, please make it payable to **Peak Experience Art & Publishing.**

☐ To charge your order to a major credit card, please fill in the information below:

Charge to: ☐ Visa   ☐ Mastercard

Account No._____

Expiration Date_____

Signature_____

Send your payment with this order form to:
   Peak Experience Art & Publishing
   P.O. Box 2116
   Santa Rosa, CA 95405-0116
   (All prices subject to change without notice. Please allow 4-6 weeks for delivery.)